TWILIGHT

AT

TIKAL

TWILIGHT
AT
TIKAL

by

John Scherber

The Eighteenth Book in the Murder in Mexico
Series

San Miguel Allende Books
San Miguel de Allende, Guanajuato, Mexico

ACKNOWLEDGMENTS

Any book starts as an idea, and by its completion becomes a joint effort.

Thanks to the following:
Lander Rodriguez for the cover design.
Julio Mendez for website design.

For editing and many valuable suggestions: my wife, Kristine Scherber.

Cover painting by the author.

This is a work of fiction. Any resemblance to actual persons, living or dead, is entirely coincidental.

ISBN: 978-0-9906551-6-9

San Miguel Allende Books
www.sanmiguelallendebooks.com

Also by John Scherber

FICTION

(The Paul Zacher Murder in México mystery series)

Twenty Centavos

The Fifth Codex

Brushwork

Daddy's Girl

Strike Zone

Vanishing Act

Jack and Jill

Identity Crisis

The Theft of the Virgin

The Book Doctor

The Predator

The Girl from Veracruz

Angel Face

Uneasy Rider

Lost in Chiapas

The Jericho Journals

Noble Rot

The writer's job is twofold: to be first of all a storyteller, and second, to ferret out the truth and fearlessly declare it to a world burdened with lies.

—Derek Hamilton, *A Philosophy for Our Time*.

For Kristine

CHAPTER ONE

*Y*ou *don't know me, Mr. Zacher,"* the letter began in a firm, almost elegant hand, *"but I learned about your services from one of your former clients. Although she asked me not to use her name, she told me she'd had a very positive experience with the Paul Zacher Agency a few years back."*

A rather formal beginning, I thought, and not the style of anyone very young. Setting it to one side I again studied the front of the grayish blue airmail envelope with its four rows of short diagonal red and blue stripes lining the borders. These days it's rare to receive a regular paper letter that isn't a bank statement or an ad from some business. This one bore two real postage stamps and the postmark was dated four days ago in Guatemala City, Guatemala, where the return address was the Hotel Goya. In its design and texture it felt like an artifact from the 1940s, as if it had fallen out of somebody's stamp album or scrapbook of mementoes. I didn't mind that; I often prefer retro things myself.

"We don't know anyone in Guatemala, do we?"

I said to Maya Sanchez, my partner in life and in the Zacher Agency. I had been reading aloud to her as we sat outside having breakfast in our vine-covered loggia at the edge of the garden at our house in central México. The rest of the mail—the Telmex phone bill, a flyer from la Comer supermarket, and a monthly statement from a local bank account we had closed more than a year earlier, was waiting unopened on the end of the table. I knew from prior mailings that the bank account statement showed we still had thirty-four centavos left in the account, less than two cents in American money. The one in my hand was the only envelope that had looked interesting enough to examine more closely.

On that brilliant day in mid April the weather was warm and welcoming, even at 6,400 feet here in San Miguel de Allende in the mountainous center of the country. Our banana tree, after struggling through the mild winter, was beginning to find a reason to live another year, although how many bananas it would decide to produce was still an open question. Often it seemed to survive here under protest.

Maya put her finger to her lower lip. "I don't think we do know anyone that lives there. Who would be the woman client that recommended us? Usually our clients have been men. Most women prefer not to have the kind of problems we take on."

"But yet there was your friend, Marisol Cross, on

our first case," I said. That had been seventeen clients ago, when we were almost unwillingly drawn into this business. We'd filed that case as *Twenty Centavos*, and there were some dark reasons for remembering it all too well.

"And Liza Carver in the Yucatán case," she added. With good reason we had filed that outing as *The Predator*.

"Right, and then we were working for Barbara Watt in Oaxaca," I said. "The case with all that Aztec gold that was cast into the shape of a human skull."

"We haven't seen her in a while." Maya looked relieved as she dredged up the last of the yogurt on her plate with a wedge of pineapple.

"Sometimes I miss her, though." I looked off neutrally into the bromeliads, although nothing about Barbara Watt could be called neutral. Somewhere out there among the random cover of sago palms and hibiscus, I knew that Orlando, our long-tailed garden grackle, was listening to this with interest. He always displayed the veiled movements of a spy, although I don't think he has the mental capacity to be one. Being a good mimic isn't always enough.

"I'm sure you do miss her. Barbara was gorgeous and she could never keep her hands off you."

"In that way she was almost Mexican, but she was also a fan of my painting. It did send a certain message."

"And I sent one back to her." With a satisfied smile Maya set down her empty coffee mug with a focused impact on the wooden plank table.

"I guess that's why we haven't seen her in a while."

Written on onionskin paper so thin it practically drooped over my fingers, the letter from Guatemala carried the old-fashioned aura of a black and white movie, possibly one featuring Humphrey Bogart and Sydney Greenstreet. I spread it out and started reading again.

"Your website informs me that you have handled some missing persons work in the past. My current problem concerns my nephew, Darren. He's thirty-seven years old and the son of my late sister, Nora. I suppose you could say I'm his guardian now, although I would never have thought he needed one until he disappeared here in Guatemala not too long ago. Perhaps I should start at the beginning.

"From the little I've been able to put together thus far from others, it all began to turn bad for Darren during a rough night in Antigua, where he had lived for several years."

"That phrase has an interesting ring to it, and Antigua does sound familiar," I said, "but I can't place it. Is it a historic town of some kind?"

Maya was a historian by trade with a master's degree from her hometown university, UNAM in Mexico City, and she knew something about Central America, which had briefly remained part of México until right after the War of Independence of 1810-21. San Miguel de Allende, where we live, is a historic town that played a role in that conflict much like Lexington and Concord had in the States. It's the place where the War of Independence began. She was nodding.

"I was in Antigua for two weeks with my family about ten years ago, when I had just turned twenty. It's an old colonial settlement, founded the same year as San Miguel, 1542. Until an earthquake wrecked it some time in the 1770s it was the capital of Guatemala, which was then just another province in New Spain, as México was then called. It also has its own volcano. San Miguel is a bigger town, though."

Here we have about 75,000 people, and that includes a colony of eight or ten thousand American and Canadian expats. Usually they make up our principal client base, but apparently, not this time.

"I wonder if Guatemala is a tough place," I said. "We don't hear much about it."

Maya looked at me solemnly. "Any place can be tough if you're not careful. Of course, it's not like Honduras, the most dangerous place in the hemisphere."

I picked up the letter again. "I'm surprised we're not being asked to look at a case there."

"My nephew Darren had gone for a meeting that night at The Blue Gazelle. That was five weeks ago. None of his friends ever saw him again—and I've tried to talk to all of them, at least

the ones I could find. I came up here from Panama City ten days ago at the request of his girlfriend, Ixobel Bak, but I haven't been able to get anywhere with this. Even though my Spanish is excellent, the police haven't been much help, although they are unfailingly polite. Even so, Ixobel doesn't have much confidence in them. I have located several private detective agencies here in the capital, but I strongly prefer one that someone I know has used and now recommends."

"Ixobel Bak?" I said. I'd pronounced the x as *sh* in what I thought of as my best Yucatán pronunciation.

Maya shrugged. "Probably. A Mayan name, I'm sure. If I remember right, Bak means flesh."

I did not follow up on this. The letter writer went on to furnish some contact information and a brief catalog of his unsuccessful efforts so far. It was mainly an itinerary of towns in Guatemala and the contacts he'd located or mostly failed to locate in each one. While the contacts were often sketchy, they still offered a place to start. I regarded them as inconsequential details with little more than potential before the writer closed with his wind up pitch.

"My friend (your former client) said you would certainly charge extra for the travel expenses. Please have no concerns about that. I possess ample means and if you take this case I would like all three of you to come down and meet with me in Guatemala City. I am offering, in addition to all expenses, twice your normal rates. Please take advantage of this, Mr. Zacher. As you can see, I don't know what else to do now. I'm sure I can no longer trust

anyone here.

"*Sincerely yours,*

"*Bernard Emerson*"

"As I now recall, people are rarely killed on missing person cases," Maya said wistfully, tucking a stray strand of hair behind her ear. "And besides, we haven't had a vacation in a while."

Having people dying around us was one of the aspects of a detective agency business like ours that she most disliked, especially when she was forced to kill them herself, as she had twice before. Vacations, on the other hand, always drew her interest.

"Not since that cult kidnapping fiasco in Chiapas last year," I said. "If you want to call what Bernard Emerson is offering a vacation, I guess the jungles of Guatemala can be quite balmy this time of year, if you bring enough bug spray." I suspected that in late April they would be steaming like a hotel and restaurant laundry in downtown Shanghai in mid August.

"Then dig your snake-proof shorts out of the armoire again, Paul darling. I think we'll have to take this case. And for once, it won't be pro bono. Señor Bernard Emerson sounds like a man of both taste and means."

"A perfect combination."

That settled it at once, since Maya is the head of the Agency that bears my name on the door.

This was a modest enough beginning to our

eighteenth case. They often are when they start in ways that belie the way they end. Our clients usually do not come to us about a shootout or a car bombing. We don't like to get involved with religious terrorists or drug cartels. I think of our business as a boutique agency that prefers to look at crimes that are more private and personal, rather than political, fanatically religious, or having their roots in business decisions, like who is going to run the drug sales in this territory. Not that they can't still become nasty and violent beyond all reason.

Cody Williams, our longtime partner in the Zacher Agency and a thirty-year veteran of the Peoria Homicide Squad, was happy to join us going south, since both football season and March Madness were finished. Baseball was starting up, but he considered that a slow game. His 230 pounds of law enforcement skill and six-foot-three height also make for better security in the field, since even when he's unarmed he presents a bigger threat than most people care to encounter face to face.

We had no other case going on and I was able to wrap up a small landscape painting I'd been working on. The great disadvantage to signing up for a long distance job like this one was that we couldn't bring our weapons on the plane, or get them through airport customs on arrival even if we had. None of us wanted to drive down to Guatemala City, although that was possible. But being unarmed always left us feeling exposed and vulnerable.

We knew that in order to get started we'd have to rearm ourselves quickly on arrival.

Two days later the three of us flew from Mexico City into Guatemala City via Interjet. Next to me sat a small, round-faced nun wearing a sky blue habit. Although that seemed like a practice outfit for Eternity, she spent much of the flight reading a long magazine article about Kim Kardashian. She traced each sentence with her finger—possibly she was practicing her English. Maya was seated across the aisle with Cody and I found some time for reflection over a couple of Finlandia vodkas on the rocks.

Of course, as Maya pointed out, not every disappearance is a murder. More often people choose to vanish because of family or financial reasons. Sometimes they're fleeing the law, escaping from an exhausted marriage or a twisted business partnership. You never know until you reach the scene, and you don't always know then. Not having ever been there, I was assuming that Guatemala was much like México in the sense that you couldn't always tell at first glance what you were looking at. Even in bright sunshine, I expected it might take a while for our vision to clear after we departed the plane.

We arrived in Guatemala City in late afternoon. The flight had taken only about two hours. We didn't have a lot of baggage and none of us looked especially suspicious, so we sailed through customs and immigration in less than half an hour.

Although Maya had remarked that this capital city had been founded the same period as San Miguel, the 1540s, coming in with our rental car we saw nothing that looked like an early colonial core, and we were staying in the old center, one block from the main square. While a few buildings were extravagantly nineteenth century in their decoration, there weren't many like that, and I saw nothing that appeared to be earlier. Even the cathedral design reflected the style of the early eighteen hundreds.

Driving in closer to the hotel, we saw a number of buildings that were scarred by peeling paint and graffiti. Many windows were boarded up. We had been told when we picked up the rental Nissan Maxima that this was not the best part of town and we ought to find secure parking for it. This turned out to be more an omen of things to come than we could ever have anticipated.

Bernard Emerson had booked us into the Hotel Goya. How handy to start our search for Darren right there, where his uncle had penned that letter. For a five-dollar bill—we didn't have any local currency yet, and dollars speak their own language almost anywhere—the concierge whisked the car away to a secure location. As the desk clerk gave us our room keys, he said that meals and drinks were included for us—we could just sign the tab and enter our room numbers. Nor did we need to worry about any gratuities. I wondered if Bernard thought we might be marking up our expenses, but we never do that. As we expected, there was also a note waiting for us at check in.

Dear Señores of the Paul Zacher Agency,

I have been required to withdraw from this hotel to another that I will not name for reasons you will soon discover. Perhaps I should not be surprised to now find myself under threat as well, much like Darren was or still is—the subject of your case. I will shortly contact you face to face to our mutual benefit. Settle in at the bar and have a drink on my tab to bring us luck. More and more I feel we're going to need it. While Guatemala is a country most pleasant in its landscape, customs, and in its people, it is also not without its darker patina of risk. Please be ready and focused on your mission. If you have not come down here prepared for violence, I hope you will find a way to arm yourselves quickly. I would not be able to sleep at night if I felt I had lost my nephew for any reason I could prevent.

He signed off with a series of normal courtesies that came from a long residence in Latin America. While in a general way I approved the tone of this missive, it seemed that his handwriting had lost some of the calculated polish of his earlier letter. It was looser and more scattered, as if, as he'd suggested, he was now under increasing stress himself. I don't like to make any judgments so early in a case, but I felt that Bernard Emerson's position was already deteriorating even as we tried to establish ours. Perhaps we should be hurrying more than we were, but until he reached us to set up an opening interview, there wasn't much more we could do other than brace ourselves for the approaching struggle.

CHAPTER TWO

After half an hour to unpack and freshen up we decided to follow Bernard Emerson's advice and reconvene in the bar downstairs. Cody was stationed in the room next to us on the third floor. The weather was noticeably warmer than at home in San Miguel, and the higher humidity gave it a subtly gentler character. Of course here we were 1400 feet lower in altitude and a little more than a thousand miles further south. Cody and I had put on short-sleeved shirts and Maya was wearing a ribbed cotton burgundy tank top with white pants and sandals. The outfit, mated with a serious look on her face, placed her mood somewhere between vacation and confrontation.

The Hotel Goya was located in the oldest part of town, and it may have looked good sixty years ago, about a block from the main plaza in Zona 1. Not that it was historic in the way you might expect from this location in a town nearly 500 years old. From the anonymous and unadorned architectural detail much of our hostelry appeared to date from the 1930s, when third rate Art Deco might've passed for cutting edge this far south.

The bathroom in our small top floor room was literally a step up from the rest of the chamber, which told me that it had been added, and the plumbing was merely overlaid on the old flooring and then floored over ten inches higher. Two drinks before bedtime would encourage you to trip over that first step during the night and stumble into the bathtub headfirst. Fortunately, Maya always traveled with a nightlight that she could plug into an outlet somewhere near the bathroom door.

The room offered two single beds of the size that required my feet to extend past the end, even though I'm only a fraction over six feet tall. Our only window didn't open and it was glazed with frosted glass. It made me wonder what the management didn't want us to see outside. And was this an indicator of Bernard Emerson's generosity? Of course, he was already paying us twice our normal hourly rate, so I didn't feel I could complain. His deposit for a $5,000 retainer had lent some credibility to our drooping bank account before we left San Miguel. This number reflected Maya's foresight. Still, we decided we'd make our own hotel reservations on the next stop and beyond.

Walking downstairs when the elevator didn't arrive after three calls, we sat at the bar and ordered drinks. Cody had a planter's punch and Maya and I had a glass of the house white wine. Waiting there in silence, we were all conscious that we needed a gun as a first priority; at least one, and preferably three. We had thought of this long before we'd received Bernard's latest note. Over the back bar a quartet of inexpensive Goya reproductions on paper were hung. I recognized two of them. One was *The Duchess of Alba* (the clothed version). Another was *The Duke of Wellington*. Nothing else in those surroundings reminded me of the great Spanish painter.

We were seated in one corner of a large covered courtyard paved with an elaborate checkerboard tile pattern. Diagonally across from us was the reception desk, and two dining rooms fronted the remaining sides. The woodwork was all old and dark brown in color, so gloomy I couldn't make out the grain. Near the bar was a life-size display of two manikins wearing native Mayan costumes. Their heads were made from inverted clay jars with the handles for ears. The overall mood was that of a tired hostelry that, while it had never been cutting edge, at least it would've appeared more welcoming between 1930 and 1960. Looking old fashioned isn't charming now if the place was never distinguished to begin with.

"I wonder what about this place spooked Bernard Emerson?" Cody said as he studied our surroundings.

"You could start with the decor," said Maya. "I wonder if someone's going to be watching us now too. I wish Bernard had said what drove him off." She glanced over her shoulder with a grim look, then scanned the two levels of the four-sided gallery above us.

"How would anyone know we were here?" I said. "You can't hack an airmail letter. Snail mail has become the safest way to communicate now, and Bernard would've just walked up to the desk in the lobby to make our reservation."

"We should've burned that letter," she said. I didn't bother to remind her that it contained a number of leads, and we hoped they would lead us to more.

The courtyard wasn't crowded. At around six-thirty in the early evening, I looked around and counted six single individuals sitting at separate tables. A siren rose and hovered on the air outside, but at some distance. There was little other traffic noise and without being sure what that meant, I had the sense that the city was in a lull. It might have been the heat.

The bartender returned with our drinks. "Will these be on Señor Emerson's tab?" he asked in perfect English as he set them down. All three of us started in surprise. Maya was the first to recover.

"Did he leave a message for us?" she said in Spanish. She never spoke English with native speakers.

He smiled broadly at her as he made a subtle gesture over our shoulders toward the far corner near the entry. At one of the circular tables under the potted palms an older man sat alone gripping a cup of coffee with both hands. As we all turned and looked that way he nodded and gestured to us in welcome. We collected our drinks and moved toward him across the courtyard. I wondered what this was about. Was it a test of some kind, like how long would it take us to find him? He looked too relaxed to be there under threat.

Bernard Emerson's broad-brimmed pale olive cloth hat was off to one side. The neck strap just visible beneath the edge suggested he was prepared for a high wind. I recognized the design; it was a hat that could travel flat in a suitcase and spring back to shape without a struggle when you pulled it out. It belonged with the gear of a man who was prepared to get around in a part of the world where he knew what to expect. He rose as we approached.

"I am Bernard Emerson," he said softly. "And you must collectively be the Paul Zacher Agency." His voice sounded educated and probably East Coast; I guessed Middle Atlantic, Maryland rather than Virginia. His grip as we shook hands was more courteous than aggressive. The business card he handed to Maya read Crossborder Trading Inc., Panama City, Panama. It did not suggest what he traded in. Maybe he was a vest-pocket dealer in exotic items that didn't leave much of a trail. I could empathize with that; we always tried to leave no footprints on the trail of evidence.

"A shrewd guess as to our identity," Cody said.

His neutral look masked a careful character scan. Long experience in law enforcement had taught him that the first meeting is often more important than many of the others. It's like a billboard that announces what the other side wants you to believe about them, more than who they really are.

"Not at all. I studied your agency's website before I wrote to you. Please take a seat. My thanks to all of you for taking on this case, and I mean that quite sincerely. I'm sure you had other things that you might have been doing."

"You're right, I could've been painting," I said, "but your wire transfer into the Agency checking account was most persuasive." Because it was a case we'd all be looking at out of the country, Maya had asked for a larger than normal deposit, in fact, ten times as much as usual.

"In this business you must've cultivated a taste for reality long ago." Emerson directed this at me more than the others.

I shook my head. "For me, not in any broader way, reality draws my attention only as it concerns finance and investigations. For the other parts of my life I prefer ambiguity and fuzzy edges. Most people have more reality than they can easily handle."

"Then that kind of flexible perspective may serve you well in this place too. I suspect you'll find this

situation with Darren as fuzzy and ambiguous as anything you've experienced lately." He sat down again after
we did.

"We had the impression that you'd been driven
off from this hotel," Cody said blandly.

"I trust that you'll forgive me that slight misrep-
resentation, but I decided I wanted to observe you in a
moment of discomfort and uncertainty at the bar, and
you have easily passed that test. There will be, I am sure,
many more to come. I've been in business for a very long
time and it is my habit to take people's measure early
when I can, if I can. Although I am well known here,
the truth is I never stay at the Goya anymore, although
I still have a dozen or so of their envelopes from the last
time I did thirteen years ago. This part of town has gotten rather too seedy for my taste in the last fifteen years. I
wanted to see how you would cope with it, because what
you're facing here in Guatemala will be no monarch but-
terfly tour in your own rural state of Michoacán."

"I can understand that," Cody said, smoothly, as
if he enjoyed this game. "It's about knowing your friends
as well as your enemies." I detected a barb in this. "So
booking us into this hotel was also part of your test?"

"Exactly. Call it an interview of sorts. This
country is not México, where by now you must be very
comfortable." Bernard Emerson smiled at us knowingly
without adding anything more. Still, he had delivered

that country name with a certain degree of disdain, as if we were still trading on the militant image of Zapata and Pancho Villa, but with little remaining substance of those times, now moldering a hundred years back. We all smiled at this reference, perhaps with less certainty. I glanced at Maya. From her rapid eye movement, she was busy sizing him up too, but she had so far offered nothing.

When he was standing as we came up to the table, I had noticed Emerson was a tall man, perhaps an inch taller than I am. Without being gaunt, his frame was spare, but not unhealthily so. His front teeth were still good, and they exhibited just enough character to convince me they were his own. His lips displayed an ambiguous livery color, one that might have been from being in the habit of either telling too much or too little, or simply from his age and exposure to tropical sunlight. I found them hard to read. I wondered whether, from his letter, we had taken him too much at face value. That's never a good thing, although I knew most people tend to accept uncritically what others say about themselves as an opening gambit. We always tried not to.

If Bernard Emerson's face truly mapped his experience, then his life must have ranged over a vast terrain, some of it rugged and uncharted. I could easily believe he was a good fit for Central America, which I have heard can be more demanding and unpredictable than México, which considers itself as much North America as is Canada. While his features were scarred, it may not have been so much from specific injuries as by the more gradual erosion or accommodation brought on by the journey through life itself. Still, this in no way suggested defeat, because that would've meant coming to rest, and the man seated across the table from us seemed to be very much in motion. The question now became where was he going with that singular momentum.

Regarding Maya with a slight smile, he stirred his coffee slowly, careful not to get any of it on the sleeve of his immaculate suit, the color of old ivory. The pale gray-blue shirt and the plain buff-colored silk tie worked well together. The ensemble unmistakably suggested a rather formal take on living in the tropics. I had no idea of the climate of Panama in the part where he lived, but being so close to the equator, it must've solely depended upon the altitude he lived at, which I knew could vary widely in that small country. He made me feel that here, in Guatemala City, we were still in what he thought of as the north. This was a broad difference in perspective, because to me, after growing up in Ohio, that phrase meant either Ottawa or Saskatoon, possibly Calgary, but still beginning well short of Yellow Knife.

"I do hope you're not in a frightful rush today," Bernard Emerson said politely, speaking through a well-used smile.

Cody smiled too. "So far we haven't noticed any-one in this country in a frightful rush, so we're happy to fit in with that pace. You're paying for our time, so we're at your disposal. What can you tell us to get this case started? Please begin anywhere. What's the most impor-tant thing that comes to mind?" From his shirt pocket he pulled out an unobtrusive notebook, smaller than the linen napkin next to his drink. The accompanying pen was short enough to be concealed in his palm, or I realized, sharp enough to be jammed into someone's throat in a tight and unexpected confrontation.

"Well, to start with, let me introduce myself more formally. You already know my name. I'm an exporter by trade and I have lived in Panama for nearly forty years. For the last five years I have no longer lived in Panama City itself, since I find that the climate there tends to wear me down. I now live in Boquete, which is more in the north and high enough in altitude to provide cool nights and welcoming mornings. At my age, I have no plans to either retire or to ever return to the United States. On those occasions when I wish to speak English, there is an adequate expat population there to humor me." He said this with a gentle smile. "While I am increasingly content with my condition, I still find myself somewhat disap-pointed in humanity, long term."

This was a broadly sketched introduction, but still

more specific than we usually received. Bernard Emerson might easily have been seventy or more, and it testified to his accumulated perspective. As I wondered what events had driven him to this point of disillusionment, I saw Cody writing that down.

"I don't think it's unusual, as we get older, to observe that in some respects the world appears to be moving beyond us. Still, when we take on a new case," Cody said, "we try to begin with a narrower focus than that. Is it something specific that is disappointing you now that you'd like us to address? Or is it life in general? Our scope of operations is not infinite. Of course, we are mainly here because of your concerns with your nephew's disappearance. Please redirect us if that's not correct."

Our employer shook his head slowly, and his tone dropped a notch. "It's not generally in my own life so much that I'm disappointed, because I've done all right in that sphere, mainly in those areas where I could depend upon myself." A frown collected more densely on his brow. "As you suggest, I am more concerned now with what's happened with Darren. As far as I could discover, it's other people who have let him down, and I still feel responsible for him, perhaps because Darren is a scholar, a longtime academic, at least at heart. My own experience in business suggests that people like him are not always sophisticated about life. They've been too insulated within the walls of their universities; do you follow me?

Sheltered from real life, they march about full of theories and ideals, even as they are protected by trigger warnings and political correctness. Therefore they can easily fall victim to the more cynical elements of society that always lie in wait for the unwary. Particularly in this part of the world." Here he shrugged and looked off toward the street. None of us commented, waiting for the bottom line. "Still, maybe your counsel to me will be to just let all this go. To stop being a fumbling old man and let the younger ones rule their own lives as well as they can. After all, it's their generation now, not mine any longer. I am willing to admit that I've had my day, and a damned good day it was. Only the cash flow still keeps me going as the emotional flow has ebbed away somewhat."

"As it would for most of us," I said. Maya could've said it better, since she paid all the bills at the end of each case. Nodding in support but not exactly approval, I settled back in my chair. "In my business I've seen plenty of that too. It's about people getting trapped by theory and remaining blind to experience, sometimes intentionally. The risk for Darren makes perfect sense if he encountered a problem he hasn't met before outside of his scholarly field. Sometimes people like that can easily get in over their heads. They need real help. Outsiders like the Paul Zacher Agency crew can often supply that best."

Bernard Emerson looked at each of us in turn. "And I can easily imagine something like that has happened here; that's why I hired you. One of the things that disappoint me most is people's ability to rationalize what they do to other people. Individuals can justify absolutely anything."

Although I agreed in a general way, I wasn't sure how to read this in Darren's case. Cody spoke as I was thinking about it. "I would have to agree, but that's not how we work in the Zacher Agency."

Had Emerson hired us and flown us down to Guatemala just to have someone to talk with as he speculated about people Darren might've encountered that were too much for him? But still, even if the old man felt the urge to generalize, he didn't seem overtly needy. According to his letter, Darren had, after all, disappeared. Was it mainly to escape conversations like this with his uncle? At thirty-seven, three years younger than I was, Darren wouldn't have yet developed most of these perspectives. Truthfully, I hadn't either, although rationalization was a major feature we saw in the players in many of our cases. Maya was studying the conversation mostly in silence. She was not given much to generalizations.

"My defense against other people's rationalizations," Cody added, "is to be an utter and brutal realist myself. I always make a point of it."

"While remaining a gentlemen, I assume, but that will be some help in this case," Emerson said, somewhat speculatively, but welcoming the general statement.

"How will this connect directly to Darren's disappearance when you get into the field?"

"It makes us astute observers," I said. "I got into this business because I was a painter, by definition a person who sees things differently."

Emerson nodded with an air of being at once both enlightened and eroded by his life's experience. "I think I understand. Everything connects, everything is interwoven, and everything is linked. I know that. But about Darren in particular, well, by training he's an anthropologist. Rather a gentleman's job, I should think, so on most days he could wear a tie. On the few times I've seen him in recent years I've never noticed any dirt under his fingernails. I understand that some anthropologists even work for large corporations now, sifting through their cultural patterns, trying to tweak them to improve their business." He made an offhand gesture as if he wasn't sure how well that worked in real life. "Darren's specialty is the culture of Mesoamerica. From where we're sitting today, that mostly means the Mayans. They make up nearly fifty percent of Guatemala's population. Do you know that indigenous group at all?" He made a broad gesture as if they were now surrounding us beyond the walls of the Hotel Goya. That was probably true, although I had heard no arrows zing overhead. I thought about this as I finished my wine. My hand went up to the roving waiter, who ignored it, perhaps because he already knew the limits of the tab Emerson was running.

"I have known more than a few modern Mayans," I said, shrugging. "Counting from when they stopped ripping people's hearts out about five hundred years ago they've since become my favorite indigenous group in all of México. They've never gotten along with the government that well, but why should they? They never got along with each other before the Spanish came, either. Within their single cultural group they have thirty-seven different languages. That alone tells you how close they wish to be. But let me shift gears. Is Darren still an academic? Or is there a college or an agency that he works for now?" I wondered whether if to stay on topic we'd have to give Emerson a somewhat shorter lead.

He shook his head slowly. "I would have to say that Darren has been freelance in that field since he finished his graduate work ten years ago. Perhaps that's an unusual condition for an anthropologist. I wouldn't know; I'm just a businessman bent on making my own way further down in the tropics."

This stopped me. Was Darren's position then like being a freelance pro football player, where you didn't need to be on any particular team? You'd sign up for a given game and then move on? A freelance city planner, where no town cared what you thought? "Do you mean he's a self-employed anthropologist? He must've inherited a substantial amount of money from your late sister." I couldn't analyze the economics of that postition otherwise.

"That is indeed possible, Mr. Zacher. I was not in any way a party to her will. She even looked elsewhere for an executor. I can't imagine why." He made a practiced gesture to the waiter, who now rushed over. "What will you all have this round?" He drew a line on the table with his finger. "We have all successfully passed the aperitif and coffee stage and we are still making some progress."

"Another planter's punch, *por favor*." This was the drink Cody often drank at home. Maya would never touch it, saying it went right to her thighs, but I'd never noticed it lingering there.

"Fine. And for me a Plantation Rum," I said, "*por favor, doble sin hielo*. Double, no ice." Emerson ordered the same.

I had come across Plantation Rum before, on our third case, one we'd filed as *Brushwork*. If it was not the best rum in the world, it was easily the best I'd ever had, and I've sampled more than a few. Emerson reached into an inner pocket of his jacket. He pulled out a small photo and set it before us in the center of the table. Unconsciously, we all leaned over at once.

"This is a picture of Darren that was taken near the end of last year when he visited me up in Boquete."

It showed a man in his mid thirties seated at a

table in a palmy restaurant. It was set with crystal and elegant silver. Three orchids floated in a bowl in the center. He had tightly curled pale reddish hair and a matching beard closely trimmed. Just lighting a cigar with a long wooden match, he wore a shirt with a floral print on a black background that might've been from the Tommy Bahama line. The contented grin on his face could have been partly explained by the exotic woman next to him with her hand possessively gripping his forearm. I placed her age at her early twenties, and she could easily have come from a Mayan background, with high cheekbones and almond eyes. Her look was intense, with small rectangular metal-framed glasses, and her hair pulled back and gathered into a severely restrained ponytail. The Mayans are not usually large people, but they can be extremely attractive. This woman clearly knew who she was. It made me wonder now even more whether Darren did. And why wasn't she now looking for him too, joining ranks with Bernard Emerson?

An odd feature of the photo was that it had not been posed. Neither Darren or the young woman was looking toward the camera, as if they didn't see the person shooting the image, and it appeared to be snapped from slightly above, as if from a nearby staircase or an otherwise modestly elevated position. Of course, Darren was absorbed in lighting that cigar properly.

"You haven't yet told me his last name," I said,

still studying the photo, wanting to ask more probing questions of our employer's view of the problem, but beyond that I needed to know much more about the missing nephew himself.

"You can keep that picture, by the way. It's Darren Hall. His mother was briefly married to his father, Jerome Hall, until he took off with a young financial analyst from Morgan Stanley. I believe that girl thought she had snagged the brains in the family. I have since heard that his principal talent lay elsewhere."

That didn't concern us. "What did your sister do for a living?"

He chuckled. "Nora ran a small hedge fund until she succumbed to a stroke at fifty-four. I believed then and I still do that it came about from all the stress the job caused her. That was fourteen years ago. Near the end she asked me to watch over Darren. He had just entered graduate school."

"Where was his father at that point?" Cody said.

"Was he out of the picture?"

"As far as I know he was never heard from again after Darren was six years old. He may be still alive for all I've ever heard, but he is definitely not available for the task before us today."

I nodded sympathetically. "Of course, and we won't need anyone's help beyond yours. Are you married, Mr. Emerson?"

"No, and now I am much too old to even go steady, since so few things are in any way steady anymore." He closed his eyes as he took a slow pleasurable swallow of the rum. I saw no surface irony in his expression, but there may have been more in his mind than I could read. But he's not too old to *be* steady, I thought. I couldn't help but smile at his remark, although I suspected he'd said it before, and more than once for the impression he knew it made.

Maya leaned forward slightly over the table. "Do you have any ideas about what might have happened to Darren? I assume he doesn't answer his emails or his cell phone when you call."

"That's right, and I have no idea. I gave you those numbers too in my letter. It's been about four months since I saw him on the occasion for the photo you now hold in your hand. He had come up to Boquete—although you might think of it as down, since he left from Guatemala—to introduce me to his new fiancé, Ixobel Bak, the young woman on his right. He paid me that kind of respect as his last family connection, the one who had guided him in getting started in his career after his mother died. He thought he and Ixobel might get married quite soon, although they had not yet set a date." Emerson shrugged. "They may be already married now without telling me. I know he felt I might be reluctant to travel because of my age. Of course that's not the case, as you can see today."

"May I ask how old you are?" Cody said.

"I'm seventy-eight."

"Could his marriagbe connected to his disap-pearance?" Maya said. "Perhaps he is simply on his honeymoon in Florianopolis or further down in South America. Not every place in Latin America has good In-ternet or cell connections."

Emerson shrugged. "I suppose, although I don't see just how he could stay totally out of touch. Why would he want to if I was his last family contact?"

I wondered silently whether that might somehow be at the core of this case. Family relations can be the basis for many stressful situations. I could bear witness to this from my own experience.

He passed me Ixobel Bak's contact information in Antigua even as he told us in the same sentence that it had not worked for him. Cody made some detailed notes as Emerson followed this with a narrative of everything he had done since he arrived in Guatemala. As the story unfolded I could see how he had traveled mostly in pur-suit of a ghost, since he had never once sighted Darren Hall in the flesh. I was also careful to write down the detail of all of the contacts and locations Emerson had visited, just to supplement the sketchy information he'd given us in his earlier letter. Although I sensed he was shrewd in some ways that might later come to light, I had no reason to trust his investigative skills. Still, I was happy to have the contacts he'd unearthed as a succession of connected starting points.

"What do you think?" he asked as he wrapped up his narrative. He drew down the last third of the rum in a single swallow. Call it relief, I thought.

"I have one more question," Cody said, folding his notebook. "What made you decide to come up here and investigate his disappearance yourself? I assume that took some time away from your business."

Bernard Emerson gave him a slow and thoughtful grin, at once humorless and subtly veiled.

"A sense of urgency began to grow on me. Late in February, he emailed me and asked that I send him a book from my collection. You see, I have rather a large library of historical and archaeological documents relating to Central America. It's a passion of mine, I suppose, although I'm not by any means a scholar in the way Darren is."

"Couldn't he have found that book online?" said Maya, never an easy sell.

"Not this particular one." Emerson took a thoughtful look at his glass and gestured to the now hovering waiter. "It was a privately printed journal of the researches of an amateur archaeologist in the nineteen-sixties. I'm sure there must be other copies about, and it's not worth much, but you wouldn't ever find its contents online."

"What was it called?" I said.

"It was titled *My Search for the Death Masks of the Mayan Late Classic Period*, and the author was Sylvan Roberts. I know absolutely nothing else about him, and I've searched the record. He may even have been an amateur; field research was much less formal back then. I came across the book at an estate auction about fifteen years ago. I became alarmed when it was returned to me undelivered after I sent if off to Darren by DHL. I had sent it to his address in Antigua, the one I sent you, and they had tried to contact him unsuccessfully several times. When I couldn't reach him by phone or email, it was then that I started researching his whereabouts. I wasn't able to get away from Panama immediately because of some business concerns, but I'm not sure that arriving here any sooner would've helped."

"Did he say why he wanted to see that book?" I said. "That sounds more like archaeology than anthropology."

"You could be right about that, but I don't know his reasoning. Sadly, I was never around him as he was growing up in New York, and I wish I had gotten to know him better. Does this sound like something you can handle?"

I put on my game face. "I can always promise our best effort. That's a given. Any outcome involves a broader field and a chancier one, especially when we're off our home turf. We will do everything we can to find Darren. You saw that in the disclaimers we sent you. Frankly, you're buying the effort more than the outcome. Our best effort can always be guaranteed but the result can never be."

"But don't ever think we're not still damn good," Cody said. "We'll start with this first name on your list, Luis Figueroa."

"Yes, as you can see from the address, he's a banker with Banco Comercial here in town on Reforma. I've used him twice myself for Crossborder Trading, and in the past Darren has handled a few transactions with me through Luis. It was mostly field equipment and credit lines for his work."

"And you've talked to Figueroa about us already?" Cody said.

"Yes, and I've told him to feel free to talk to you, within the limits of what his business will allow. I felt you might want to ask him some questions I haven't thought of, anything you can come up with. I can imagine that you never know just where information of value might turn up."

When Bernard Emerson rose to say goodbye I realized he had hung a cane over the back of his chair. I hadn't noticed it when we joined him. After a minute's delay, we walked out of the Hotel Goya courtyard bar and restaurant with five pages of Cody's notes and the single page contact list from Emerson. I had jotted down a number of ideas of my own. The case was shaping up to be a lot of ground level sniffing on a trail that was rapidly growing cold. Once in the street I decided that what we needed most was context for the next phase of this investigation. I called Luis Figueroa on his cell phone and set up an appointment for the following morning. He sounded surprised and not entirely pleased to be reached at home on a business matter.

While Maya and I talked to him the next day Cody planned to head for the city market to buy a trio of black market guns and some ammunition if he could get it. From everything we'd heard about Guatemala City as a risky place, we all felt confident that he'd be able to pull it off. Weren't the street gangs getting their weapons from somewhere? From the police presence on the streets I could imagine the armed cohorts that would be required to protect a legitimate gun store, if they even existed.

While nothing about this case so far looked easy, at least we were in motion.

CHAPTER THREE

As I reread these notes it seems like I've portrayed Guatemala City as a tough town. Without having a detailed set of reasons to think so, that was still the impression it made on all of us. Not that we hadn't worked in difficult situations before. On the case we filed as *Strike Zone*, the city of Oaxaca that season was in the grip of a massive teachers' strike that had turned terribly violent. We'd also solved a high society murder in *Brushwork*, where the victim was a former Vice President of the United States murdered during an exclusive social occasion. In any case, while Guatemala City might be tough, I'm still not suggesting it's the sister city to Chicago.

On the morning after our talk with Bernard Emerson, Maya and I emerged onto Sixth Avenue at about 9:30, looking both ways before we closed the door behind us. Cody had left an hour earlier. Without guessing his intentions, the armed tourist police, stationed four on each side of every block in the central district, had kindly pointed him in the direction of the city market.

Maya and I walked toward Avenida La Reforma where Luis Figueroa was expecting us around ten at the Banco Comercial. Under a clear and promising sky, the traffic was dense and noisy. The principal means of communication among drivers was by laying on the horn. Motorbikes and bicycles threaded their way through the herd with an air of being shielded by their own immortality. Helmets were a luxury few could afford. The three I saw were all hanging like status trophies from the handlebars. The sidewalk traffic around us sometimes looked edgy, and Maya gripped my arm. Neither of us had brought any money, leaving it locked in the room safe with our passports. I can't begin to say how much we missed being armed. As for Maya's wish that this trip might have some vacation overtones, she had not mentioned that again.

Many of the buildings were disfigured by graffiti and I didn't see any signs of an attempt to scrub it off. Call it local color.

"I feel like we've learned some new things about Guatemala," she said. "But that's not helping me understand any of this now that we're here. How does this town work? How can people get anything done when they're looking over their shoulder all the time? Even Mexico City was never like this before the authorities cleaned it up."

"Maybe it's partly the legacy of the civil war," I said. "It was thirty-six years of conflict following the CIA overthrow of the government. People learned to value their guns."

She only shook her head. Fifteen minutes later we came up before the entrance of the Banco Comercial. The building had a look that was common on Reforma. It was the fortress style of the 1970s, a frowning beetle-browed kind of architecture. Repeated on both sides of the street, ten to fifteen stories high with deeply recessed windows surrounded by stone and precast concrete, its message was that we are ready to repel street protests at any time. This look was also mimicked in that period in many large cities in the United States.

In the lobby the decor was what would've been called modern thirty years ago, as expressed by a lot of well-used black leather and chrome furniture in the waiting area. I felt as if we were there to apply for a loan, if information could be loaned out. After a five-minute wait, Maya and I were ushered into a small office to meet Luis Figueroa.

Our banker was a small man of about forty, my age, wearing a straw-colored tropical suit that even that early in the day smelled of cigar smoke. Some of the odor may also have been coming off his luxurious moustache. His thick black hair was carefully oiled and came to a point in a widow's peak. In that very ethnic town his skin was as white as Maya's, who had never acknowledged being more than two percent Aztec, and even then only after three glasses of wine. She never smiled when I suggested she'd look good in a feather outfit.

When he had stood to greet us coming in I judged Luis Figueroa's height to be about five-foot-seven, no more. That also would be typical for most of the men we'd seen in the streets as we walked to the bank. He would've thought himself to be average height, as he locally was.

"Please sit down," he said, speaking in English after we introduced ourselves. He made a gesture toward the glass front of his office and a young woman in a tight black skirt and a starched white blouse entered with a tray bearing cups and a carafe of coffee. "I understand from Señor Emerson (he pronounced this as *Aimairsone*) that you are here to assist him in *deescobering* the current location of Señor Darren Hall."

"Exactly. We are hoping you can help us to do that," Maya said in Spanish, with no special inflection. She appeared to have little interest in flirting with this man. I made a mental note to ask her why later, since that was a departure from her normal style.

"What I have done for Señor Hall three or four times in the past is to arrange certain transfers of money from his account here to other accounts in Guatemala, not always his own."

"Were these transfers made in quetzales?" I said. This was the domestic currency, named for the national bird and rather inflated in value, as if in perpetual flight, I thought, against the dollar. The local banks wouldn't take Mexican pesos in exchange for it.

"Always. In every case Señor Hall wished to avoid the currency tax, and we were able to help him do that." We had been told that often transactions going through the local banks involving dollars were subject to a federal tax of twelve percent. Luis Figueroa's wide smile displayed a prominent gap in the center of his upper teeth. He could've nearly put a straw through it without reducing its flow by much.

"Can you tell us who received these transfers?" I said lightly, as if it were of no great importance.

He paused to take a long sip of his coffee. "Unfortunately, no, since our rules of confidentiality prohibit releasing that information except to the Security Police. I am sure you will understand why. Similarly we cannot reveal the amounts, although I am eager to help you in any way I can."

"Of course," I said bleakly. Why the hell had Emerson even bothered to give us this man's name? Was it only to show us the kind of roadblocks he'd encountered?

"I can see you are a creative person," Maya said, after a thoughtful pause, studying a drab modern semi-abstract floral painting on the wall behind him. We could just make out the signature in the lower left corner. It said *L Figueroa*. Christ! I said to myself. Another bloody painter.

The banker bowed from his neck. "In my garden I am the king, as you would say." He made an offhand gesture toward the painting. "It inspires me to portray what I grow."

"Indeed, not everyone would be able to paint like that," I said. It was the most heartfelt statement I'd been able to make in his office thus far.

"Of course," Maya added. "And kings will make their own rules, but I am also sure that, without offering anything that would violate your bank's policies of disclosure, your more dominant creative instinct could still find a way to send us on to another point of contact with Señor Darren Hall. We feel his life may be at risk here. In México Señor Zacher and I are known as humanitarians from our record of saving the lives of other people, so there is some reason to hurry." Avoiding his eyes, as if her frank look required something more, she lifted her cup to her lips while she contemplated his response.

When he paused to consider this, I added, "As we have said, we are investigators working for Bernard Emerson." Not mentioning his honorific suggested how personally close we were to him and his family. "What I would hope to come away with today is another contact for Darren Hall, one that happened after yours. Of course, we don't need to mention any names. Even to give us the banking connection on the other side of one of these transfers is unnecessary. Can you, in that fertile creative ferment of your mind, which of course moves beyond the policy of this bank, a mere business, come up with a clue to send us on to the next step?"

With a narrow look, Luis Figueroa rose and reached into a file cabinet at his right. From within the reams of papers inside he came up with a file he liked. "I noticed this before, although I didn't know what it meant. Perhaps it can be of assistance to you now."

He pulled out a sheet of paper, careful to not let us see the face of it, and with a scissors, sheered off the upper third. He handed this to Maya with a gesture only marginally less than a bow.

When she passed it on to me I saw that it contained an ornate logo, a single initial embellished with curlicues and artistic figures. In my painter's eye what I saw was an M elaborated in every way possible. It could've been a royal M, as if for Lord Louis Mountbatten. Just as interesting, and perhaps more, below it in pencil was a scrawled note: *Chez Antoine, two PM*. Without comment I folded the paper in four and slipped it into my shirt pocket.

When we both met Luis' gaze with a blank look, his response was ready, again in English.

"What we say here is like they do in the USA of America, do you know this? Follow the money. *Jaja!*"

"Do you recognize who is this Antoine? And is he French?" Maya said.

Figueroa glanced over her shoulder at the waiting area and beyond.

"It is the name of a restaurant more than just a man, both the owner and the chef. In my estimation, it is an excellent place, the best in Panajachel, but some distance from here. Beyond this I cannot say. There is other business on this paper, notes if you will, from Señor Hall that I must keep with the file. If you go to find this restaurant you will greatly enjoy the lake, I believe. You cannot avoid it."

"The lake?" I repeated, thinking I should've brought our national map along.

"*Sí!* Lake Atitlán. It is a little more than one hundred kilometers west from here in the very hilly terrain. It is always popular for the *fin de semana*, the weekend as you will like to say, with your lover, you will see when you stop there." His eyes flickered back and forth between Maya and me.

"One more thing," I said. "If there is a date on that paper you clipped this from, can you share it with us?"

He nodded and reached into the file again. "January 27th, a Friday. That is all from the upper part. The rest is business, as you will understand."

That was at least something, the fragile clue snipped from the secure bank files. I would've given a great deal to have full access to that folder. Cody always traveled with his lock picks, and I knew he had them now, but they would be no help in getting us into the Banco Comercial after hours.

When Maya and I emerged into the blurred rush of traffic on Reforma, Cody was waiting for us, seated on a cast iron bench under a palm in the landscaped median with his legs crossed. As we darted across the westbound blacktop I could make out a bulge under his shirt on the right side, but only one. This was not good news. Maya sat down next to him. He was already shaking his head.

"The Mercado Central only offered a poor selection in a back room, and way too expensive, even for being illegal. I would've bought two more anyway, despite the prices, but they just wouldn't cut it. They had a Cobra .38 with a really worn action, like it had been well used in target practice. Then there was a beaten up Phoenix .22. They both looked like they'd made the rounds way too many times with little or no maintenance. And you already know I don't trust automatics very much."

"So what did you end up getting?" I said.

"A Remington .45 automatic. It looks like a U.S. Army officer's side arm. I know what I just said about automatics, and this one could be more than sixty years old, like from our invasion here in 1954, but I thought the action still looked OK. If it stayed in the hands of an old lieutenant, he might have kept it up. There were no revolvers on offer. I could try again tomorrow but I don't think we want to hang around this town any longer than we have to."

"Did you get some bullets too?" Maya said with a queasy look. "Or is it just going to be for show?"

"Twenty-one rounds that cost me about five bucks apiece. They don't look too bad. You never know until you pull the trigger, of course."

I considered for a moment what this did to our position. In the case we'd filed as *Identity Crisis* Maya had taken a shot at a suspect named Antonio Trujillo with her .32 automatic as he exited our front door, running. She missed him. Cody killed him later after he came within a centimeter of killing Maya and me. We never talked about it much, but that recollection didn't give me any reason to entrust this .45 to her. I wasn't a bad shot, but Cody had all the experience. He'd killed four people in his police career, which gave him the kind of credibility we needed now. I recalled that this was only a missing person case, but Guatemala already looked like a danger-ous field of operation to go around in armed only with good manners and an easy grin.

Maya had reached the same conclusion. "I guess our lives are in your hands now." She gave him a bleak smile.

He placed his hand over her wrist. "They always have been." The traffic rushed on by, unaware of this tipping point. "I'll show it to you later, when we're back at the Goya."

I looked at him with a steady gaze. "How do you feel about our position now?"

"Cautious, alert, cool. I don't ever allow myself to get nervous, even when I should. Nervousness messes with your aim. Of course, you don't want to get too happy, either. Calm and neutral is always the best way to be." Maya and I could both see that this was as much reassurance as we were likely to get from Cody in the case of the missing Darren Hall. As we waited for an infinitesimal gap in the traffic before streaking back across the pavement, I reminded myself again that such cases aren't always that dangerous. Eight blocks away we found ourselves on Sixth Avenue again and we turned toward the Hotel Goya. In the traffic noise Maya and I held back from telling him about Luis Figueroa.

About halfway there, on a section of the pavement blocked to vehicle traffic, we heard a sudden yelp among the crowd of pedestrians. We all wheeled around. A young woman with a baby in her arms was rising from the street, cradling the infant's head against her breast. Gripping a cell phone in his left hand, a kid in his late teens leaped away from her toward another woman, this one a blasé tourist with sandy blond hair and a slender build. As he caught up with her a second later, he hooked her pendant and chain with two fingers and yanked them off her neck. But her hand was as fast as his, and with an ugly grimace she caught it too. They both went down thrashing on the pavement. She punched him sharply in the face as she held onto the chain with her other hand.

He staggered to his feet and so did she an instant later, but he was now in motion again, rushing our way, skirting the crowd that had now nearly all turned toward him and against him. With no warning, Cody took two long strides out into the middle of the street quicker than I thought he could move, and the kid careened into his immovable mass, full speed at the hip, and was thrown backward onto the pavement, momentarily stunned.

The blond woman thrust her arm into the air, the pendant still swinging from her fingers. "You didn't get my mother's diamond, you filthy bastard! You got nothing from me!"

I would've said something stronger, but in that instant three other kids from the crowd jumped onto the dazed runner and pinned him down before he could get to his feet. One was kneeling on his chest gripping his throat. The cell phone skittered away back toward its owner. Four armed tourist police surged toward us from the end of the block, drawing their guns, and we walked calmly on. For the Paul Zacher Agency, it was just another day in the big city.

"I guess the locals are getting a little tired of this, too," I said. We reached the Hotel Goya five blocks later.

When we paused at the front desk to collect our room keys Maya turned to Cody. "I hope you packed your Speedo," she said. "We're going to the lake tomorrow."

We changed upstairs and came back down for lunch in the hotel to talk about our conversation with Luis Figueroa during a time when we could include a little more detail. Although we all thought of ourselves as somewhat hardened to crime, none of us was sorry at the thought of moving on from Guatemala City.

CHAPTER FOUR

As a native of northern Illinois, growing up on the edges of the wooded lake country of the Upper Midwest, from early childhood Cody must've understood that phrase, "Going up to the lake." It was idiomatic of summer vacations, the promising blaze of July sunlight, followed by fireflies at dusk. It meant seasoned wooden rowboats rocking against the old tires that guarded the sides of the creaking dock, and outboard motors with a battered gas can, bamboo fishing poles for the kids and fly rods for the grownups. It called up the image of painted lures, crimped lead sinkers and bait—minnows and night crawlers. It was coasting up to the peeling white-painted dock at the end of the afternoon with your daily limit aboard of sunfish and perch, maybe a northern pike or two. You would be sunburned, perforated by mosquito bites, and more than ready for a tall cold one well back from the fire pit when dusk settled in around the cabin.

But on the Guatemala westbound highway the

following morning, what we discovered was not a good fit for such Norman Rockwell images of a high summer's day edged by a forest of lush pines. Although Lake Atitlán was only about one hundred and seven kilometers— sixty-four miles away, the road was contorted by one hairpin curve after another. The view of the rear quarter of black-belching dump trucks was a sight far more common than any natural features. Many of the steep hillsides had been carved away to feed cement plants and crush gravel from the slabs of limestone. What would've been an hour's trip on a good road and level ground was three and a half hours of swaying back and forth, stopping and starting. Carsick travelers would need to have their windows open all the time. Fortunately, none of us were. We'd gotten started about nine o'clock and we soon realized it was looking like a late lunch ahead.

After the rush of the capital traffic cleared, the occasional small towns looked like they'd all been conceived on the same pattern. They were cobbled together with whatever was available, and if there hadn't been enough of one material to finish a façade, anything else would be patched in. The money had always run out before any sense of charm or esthetics could be thought of. It made me reflect on how beauty was an unavailable luxury for people who were only scratching to get by. Yet the embroidered fabrics we glimpsed in these tiny markets were ablaze with color and originality. As a painter,

I already knew that the creative life offers redemption from the vicissitudes of daily existence. What I was seeing as I passed only confirmed this view.

Further on, the drop-offs alongside of our rented Nissan were dizzying. We studied the sky as raptors circled in straggling groups hoping for our first wrong turn. "As the tenderest they'll eat you first," I said to Maya. "I do take some consolation in that, although I'll miss you."

"As the toughest, I'll be the last," Cody said, rather smugly.

Finally we were able to catch a glimpse of Lake Atitlán below, patches of languid blue between breaks in the mutilated landscape. Not that it hadn't been self-mutilating as well, even beyond the devastation provided by excavators. I had done some research online before we left the Goya. As I learned, Guatemala inconveniently rested athwart the junction of two tectonic plates that got along about as well as the Democratic and the Republican parties in even-numbered years. The result was a process of unceasing upheavals that rent the landscape into a ruinous condition often appreciated as picturesque, but one of unpredictable misery for the residents trying to cross a street that had been there when they'd gone to bed, but no longer when they went to work the next morning. We are all creatures of habit, I thought, and that exhibits our worst vulnerability in a world as unpredictable as this. I realized that much of the beauty around us came from inconceivable violence. What I loved most about painting (when it went well) was its tranquil, effortless flow. I made a note to consider this later in more detail.

And then, like the Promised Land, the larger vista of Lake Atitlán came broadly into sight within a long, ragged gap in the scarred framing landscape. From my research, I already knew it was formed from a caldera in the far distant past, the blown out crater of an enormous volcano. While geological timetables run at once in eons and époques, and vastly indifferent to human needs, here was a real presence, a forceful relic that was both dominant and undeniable. Its current peaceful mood must be an illusion, I thought, an uncharacteristic instant of tranquility embedded in a fabric of more dependable chaos.

The collective exhaust valve for this subterranean turbulence was a collection of volcanoes second to none. As we curved downward toward the water I could see three of them positioned along the far shore.

For a while we were almost speechless. Small swathes of cloud curled near the top of each one. Or was it a mixture of smoke and steam?

"What in God's name was Darren Hall looking for in this place?" Cody said.

"A late lunch or *comida*, just like we are," Maya said in a businesslike tone, pulling out the scrap of letter paper we'd gotten from Luis Figueroa. "*Chez*

Antoine, two PM, and then there's this funny emblem, this elaborate M."

Bernard Emerson's notes had also mentioned a restaurant in Panajachel, but he hadn't been able re-member the name of it. "I'm sure you'll be able to figure it out once you're on the ground there," he said, "if this takes you that way."

After another half hour the twisty road leveled off and we found ourselves cruising into the edge of Panaja-chel. The traffic was not troublesome, an odd mixture of cars, pickups, but mostly tuc tucs—three-wheeled taxis with seating for two on a bench seat in the back. The top and the partial sides were fashioned of fabric and clear plastic stretched tightly over a tubular metal frame. They would provide marginal protection from the weather and none at all from collisions.

As we approached the lake, Panajachel looked like a town that existed only for the tourist trade, to my mind not a real place. Still, with a kind of gritty chaotic reality, it was definitely more cheerful and lively than the struggling towns we'd recently passed through. The In-ternet had told me it held less than 12,000 people and was situated at a little higher than 5,000 feet. The streets were packed with trinket and craft shops, restaurants and bars, small *tiendas* hawking wine and snack foods. Com-ing in we noticed several decent-sized hotels, and Maya had booked us into the Park Hotel del Lago. This was a six-story hostelry within view of the beach. We were on the fifth floor next to Cody and all the rooms had tiny concrete balconies that faced the water and the looming volcanoes to the west. At one o'clock we met in the lobby and left in search of Chez Antoine.

By scanning the two or three main streets we found it on Calle Santander. The restaurant was not a large place. The indoor seating in the front was composed of half a dozen tables with a bar along the side offering four stools, and through a pair of French doors, a garden court offered five more tables, each with an umbrella. The detail was thoughtful, with potted geraniums everywhere and light fixtures with a European bistro flavor. The napkins were good linen. Only one table was occupied.

When we entered, a middle-aged man in a crisp chef's jacket came over and welcomed us in English as he led us to our seats. His accent sounded almost German, but not conventionally so. Perhaps Austrian or Swiss, I thought. His consonants were subtly softer; I've always had an ear for that. His nametag read Franz Anton Weibel. That's where he got Antoine, I thought.

"Another exile," said Cody as our host moved away to get our drinks. He and I both also thought of ourselves in that way with no regrets, even though Guatemala seemed like a foreign country after our long years in México. Maya just called us gringos and shrugged whenever our status came up in our conversations, which it rarely did.

"Now I'm imagining Darren Hall sitting in this chair with someone else for lunch at two P.M. on January 27th," said Cody. "This is the jumping off point into a situation that results in his disappearance."

"I don't get it," I said. "He's lived in Guatemala for years, so I don't see what charm this place would have for him, not this restaurant specifically, but this town."

"Maybe he's meeting a woman here," said Maya, "and because it's so far from any place where you'd expect to find him, he doesn't risk Ixobel finding out."

"He's researching the tribal habits of resort places," said Cody, "the collective mindset of people who sell overpriced gewgaws to strangers day after day. The rituals they use to maintain their self-respect."

"The kind of twisted crimes they commit to amuse themselves," I suggested. Perhaps we needed our own anthropologist to study the habits of private detectives early in a new case when they had too little to go on to enable them to talk any sense. The conversation continued in this vein as we ate.

When we were nearly finished the chef returned to check on our meal.

"Delightful," I said. "It's great to find real European food in Guatemala." I wasn't sure which European enclave this represented.

Weibel bowed slightly with a satisfied look. "You are on a tour now here?" he said.

"Not exactly." Maya pulled out the photo of Darren Hall with his fiancée and handed it to him. "We were supposed to meet a friend of ours here in Panajachel but now we can't find him. We came here today because he had talked to us about this place as one he enjoyed and we hope you might recall seeing him. Perhaps you would even know where he's staying. His name is Darren Hall, and the woman with him is Ixobel Bak. She may have been here too."

Our sun umbrella was furled and the table was shaded by a grape arbor that had grown in coverage as the afternoon progressed. As Weibel stepped to one side and angled the photo into better light a wrinkle creased his brow. He started to nod. "Yes, as I believe, I did see this man, because I do remember the crinkly hair so red in color. We don't see it that much here. But he did not tell me his name, and this woman was not with him then, I think."

"Was he here alone?" Cody said, staring at quite a good parrot painting on the wall near the French doors, as if this question didn't greatly matter. He knew as much about painting as he did about crocheting doilies. Still, I made a note to check the surface characteristics of that picture as we left. I always find brushwork interesting.

"No. I believe he was seated with another man at

that time; let me consider this now for a little. I will come back to you."

Franz Anton Weibel moved to another table to take a drink order. It may have been that at this time of day in light traffic, he handled the floor by himself. He appeared to be a man who surveyed the detail of his restaurant with Teutonic precision. Fortunately for us, that included the current and former patrons. However, if anyone came along in a few days tracking us, we could expect no confidentiality.

Ten minutes later, after taking care of the only other occupied table, Weibel returned with a sheet of paper in his hand. He presented it to Maya and she spread it out in front of her. It showed a scan of two checks made out to the restaurant, and next to each was a driver's license.

"You accept checks here?" Cody said, surprised.

"Yes, Guatemala checks if the people have the Guatemala driver's license. For each one I make a copy like this for my records. You can keep it since it is a duplicate I just made."

The uppermost check was from Darren Hall, drawn on the Banco Comercial, but not from the headquarters in Guatemala City. It was from a branch in Antigua. The license next to it showed Hall without the beard. His address was also listed as the place in Antigua I recognized from Emerson's information. It bore a date in the last week of January.

The other check was drawn on the account of Theodore Asher, a name we hadn't heard and which did not appear in Bernard Emerson's notes. The bank didn't matter but his home address was in a town called Flores. Asher looked around forty years old with a narrow intense face and loose curly brown hair. Any more was hard to make out since these license photos were barely more than an inch high. The amount of both checks was between 160 and 190 quetzales—around twenty dollars or a bit more.

"Does this Asher name mean anything to you?" Cody asked.

"No, but both the checks cleared the bank with no problem, and I did not see those men again. Neither of them was a regular customer."

From her purse Maya pulled the paper we'd gotten from Luis Figueroa. "Does this emblem mean anything to you?" It was the elaborately embellished M.

Weibel gave her a long look that slowly evolved into a smile. "No, it does not. And this is not just about looking for an acquaintance you expected to meet here, is it, my friends?" Not expecting an answer, he moved away. Subtlety will only take you so far, I thought.

Cody waited until our host returned to the kitchen before speaking. "Where is Flores?"

Maya had already pulled out her phone and hit

the maps app. "It's in the Petén, the northern part of the country. Not very close to this town, sadly." She slid the phone across the table to Cody.

"So why is Theodore Asher down here meeting with Hall?" I said. "If it's such a long way from home? This is the southwestern part of the country."

A delicate curl appeared on Cody's lips. "I think I know."

"What?" Maya said.

"Darren Hall is chasing something. Trust me, I can feel it."

"Why would he be chasing something that would make him disappear?" I said.

"Something that would make him disappear only if he found it," Maya said. "Maybe Darren Hall wanted to disappear because he had."

CHAPTER FIVE

After lunch Cody disappeared into his fifth floor room. Maybe he was oiling that .45 automatic, or it could've been that he wanted to take a nap to prepare for what was coming. Maya and I headed for the pool. Taking our time, we rubbed some sunscreen on each other. The only other swimmers there were a French-speaking couple with two teenage boys.

"What do you think Darren Hall is up to?" she said, kneeling beside me as she finished working on my back. "We never got a real sense from Bernard Emerson of what a free lance anthropologist might do to make a living. There aren't that many choices in this country that I've seen. For industries you've got tourism, agriculture and...and..."

"Crime," I said, taking her left foot in my hand and carefully rubbing the sunscreen between her toes. She could've done that herself but we both preferred that I do it. "Like Cody suggested, Hall is chasing something, and it's probably not coffee beans, coconuts, or pineapples. He's not running a tour service, because he'd have to advertise it and I haven't been able to find the slightest trace of him on the Internet. It's as if he's not quite real."

"And he's not driving a chicken bus, I would think," she added, pinning her hair up so I could work on the back of her neck. Although she loved the radiant glow of the sun, like most Mexicans, she was terrified of darkening her skin.

Looming over us across the lake were the three volcanoes. I couldn't look at them anymore without thinking of Pompeii and Herculaneum, or Mount Saint Helens. They could turn cranky at any time and start an unfortunate ruckus. They also reminded me of Popocatepetl, the ever ready, seething volcano overlooking Puebla back in México. At about 4:30 we crossed to the bar for a piña colada to cool off. The answers to some of these questions about Darren were going to be found more easily on the road.

We didn't linger much longer in Panajachel, pleasant as it was in a Latino Coney Island fashion. It was crammed with altogether too many tourists, too many gewgaws, too many shops selling crafts that made me wonder how many times they'd been marked up on their way there from what the indigenous people had gotten when they first sold them. Most prominent was the *huipil*, the standard pullover sleeveless women's top that everyone sold. Most of them were beautifully designed and executed. We'd seen them around San Miguel in a variety of decorative uses, and not only as apparel. People at the front desk of the hotel counseled us that the best prices and selection could be found over the hills in Chichicastenango, where the markets on Thursday and Sunday were legendary. Nodding politely, instead we headed north-by-northeast when we left the next morning, striking out toward the steamy heart of the Petén. The only thing of interest we took away with us was the name and address of Theodore Asher, whatever that might be worth. It was like a piece of string, a fragment of a filament we knew was much longer, and string always has direction. Now so did we.

Why had Darren Hall met Theodore Asher in that lakeside town? Because they both lived in Guatemala they would've known exactly what they were looking at. I doubted they were they shopping for expensive *huipiles*. From the information we saw on their checks at Chez Antoine, Asher was a very long way from his home in Flores, and if Darren's home in Antigua was not so terribly far off, I still didn't see anything to interest an anthropologist in the gaudy huckster-driven streets of Panajachel. Some of these distances that were two-thirds of the way across the country were not that vast in terms of kilometers, but the driving speed through the twisted and unforgiving terrain was much slower than you would expect, and often no more than a crawl. Good roads were not plentiful, and they understandably drew most of the traffic wherever they appeared. The rest lacked passing lanes and were clotted with slow-moving vehicles. Dump trucks often outnumbered cars.

Pulling away from the lakeside hotel, we were braced for an all-day drive through the land where the chicken bus, the kind Maya had mentioned at the pool, was king of the road. The local informal counterpart of Trailways or Greyhound, the chicken buses are a vast collection of independent transports that are enthusiastically repainted, rechromed, and embellished, and fitted with bright steel racks on the top. They've been largely created from resuscitated American school buses that (as it was so naively believed in the States) have exhausted their useful life. In this condition they've been cheaply sold into an underground railway running south into the heart of the Guatemala jungle. There they have taken on a second wind, a rock and roll old age clinging to the uncertain sides of the highways of Guatemala. While many are crowded with openwork boxes of chickens on the top, any other cargo will do as well. You can put your plywood bass fiddle up there, your used refrigerator, a sack of mangoes, or the body of your mother-in-law on the way to a distant burial in her hometown in Belize. Everything is practical in Guatemala.

This system is the most visible element of the interstate transport complex of this country, and it is managed with a great deal of flair and bravado. Here style and flamboyance have replaced capital, always in much shorter supply. As I had several times observed in walking past when they were parked, the interiors of these vehicles had not been given the same degree of loving restoration, and the term *bench seat* was equally literal and unforgiving. It was possible that the undersides of the cushions were still dotted with nearly petrified gobs of third grade chewing gum. I was happy that we were driving our less stylish but far more rational Nissan sedan as we headed for the northern jungle.

"I can imagine we're all thinking the same thing along about now," Cody said from behind the wheel. His blithe tone suggested we knew all about what we were doing. By then we were only an hour out, still navigating the cranky S-curves.

"When has that happened before?" Maya said, seated next to him. "Remind me." She gripped the handle above the door with her right hand to keep upright. I looked at my watch, wondering if there might be some irritability already developing for this long drive.

"We all studied the maps last night," Cody continued.

"Right," I said. "Flores is in the upper middle north of the Petén country, but much lower in altitude and therefore wetter. It'll be ruthlessly steamy."

"You'll both appreciate that there's air condition-ing in the rooms where I booked us," Maya said. "They have a great pool and a bar next to it. They'll even serve you as you tread water."

"Then I'm switching to gin and tonics," I said. "That's not negotiable. It'll be Bombay Dry, not Sap-phire. I don't care what Bernard Emerson says. Main-taining morale has to be part of the overhead of this investigation too."

Cody grunted as we took a particularly tight curve. "I don't know if you looked up Theodore Asher online."

"That sounds like we should have," Maya said. "Paul and I were off duty by the pool."

"He's an expert guide, supported by a website with kind of a New Age look, almost a spiritual angle. It seems like we're going to Tikal. Why don't we just say that now outright? That whole upper Petén area is all about Tikal. There is no other reason to be there, never was. I guess that's much like it was when the ancient city flourished two thousand years ago. Flores is mainly a way of being there without living in Tikal, since it's a ruin in a national park."

"And just north of there the roads all die out," Maya added. "They end in the jungle. You can still trek into the Yucatán from along the bottom edge, like anybody would, but bring a horse to ride with a mule for your baggage, and a lot of mosquito repellant."

And snake-proof shorts, I thought. We were running too close behind a metallic violet and silver chicken bus, and the occasional feather escaped and fluttered over us. We'd seen that kind of terrain before in another case that came to earth in the Yucatán, one we filed as *The Predator*. You could not miss Maya's meaning. What was coming was the real jungle, the *selva*, as they call it here. It's a term loaded with more nuance than most people can handle.

Gradually a variety of lowland vistas interrupted the tumultuous terrain, a few valleys and river flats where agriculture was possible, first as rough pastures, then as plowed fields, with occasional flocks of sheep and cattle. After four hours the road was sloped more downward than up and the temperature was climbing point for point in competition with the humidity. The hotel had packed a lunch for us since we wanted to reach the region of Flores before dark. We munched in silence.

I found myself thinking about Bernard Emerson. What about our client's stated disappointment with reality? My observation was that if he had witnessed a great deal of rationalization on the part of other people, he had rarely been deceived by it himself. Just before we parted in the bar at the Hotel Goya, he told us he would be in Guatemala City for only two days more before returning to Panama. Then, he said, we would be on our own, but we could draw on him for additional help in any way we wished until then. It was hard to see what that might've been, I thought later as I scanned Cody's notes of our conversation.

We had not felt any need to see Bernard again, and we'd even left town before he did. For me, largely on our own was where we had always been. I was left wondering if he felt we were greenhorns, but I had lived in Latin America for eighteen years, and Maya had grown up in Mexico City before she moved to San Miguel to work on her book on the early years of Ignacio Allende, our town's revolutionary hero. Although I could readily see many differences with México, Guatemala did not look especially exotic to me, at least not so far. But of course, it was still likely to be similar to México in this regard; that it was often difficult to know just what you were looking at.

By about three o'clock that afternoon I had relieved Maya at a rest stop and was taking my shift driving on a road both leveler and straighter than any we'd seen so far. The traffic had clearly thinned as well, suggesting there were fewer reasons to be going north. We had entered the Petén an hour before. But for the agricultural clearings, the jungle was thick around us. Its character was different from the Yucatán jungle, where the topsoil over that massive limestone plateau was too thin to support large trees. There the vegetation rarely rose above eight or nine meters high, although it was often so thick you had to carve a path to walk through it.

Here the trees were much higher, many of thirty meters or more, often overlaid with networks of flowers and vines, which meant the ground was mostly shaded and the low level vegetation was much less dense. You could make your way through it without a machete, except for self-defense from snakes dropping from the branches. Whenever we slowed the car to take a more careful look the air was vivid with birdcalls. The humidity was almost so thick you could stand a toothpick on end and it wouldn't fall over. Or at least that's the way it felt.

Twenty-nine kilometers further on we passed a sign that indicated Rio La Pasión awaited us ahead. It took Maya a moment to find it on the map. In half an hour the road went into a tiny settlement, took a hard right turn, and we came to a stop behind several other vehicles. There was no bridge here, but a ferry.

The mud-colored river was broad with a sluggish current. I thought it looked shallow and about eighty meters wide. Aside from the space occupied by the village, which clearly existed only to serve the ferry, the jungle flanked the water on both banks. Odd little eddies and currents, patterned with streams of tiny bubbles, hinted at suspicious activity just beneath the surface.

It came as no surprise that the ferry was a simple enough concept. It was a flat steel deck about eight meters wide and three cars long, open to the weather. The two long sides had reassuring handrails. Beneath the closer end, secured on both sides to a short ramp, were visible the circular rims of the row of sealed steel drums that supported it. At each of the four corners were tiny pitched roofs over a projecting fixed wooden seat ahead of an outboard motor. The sides of this group of pilot-houses were screened from the weather by thin clear plastic sheets. I had to imagine that this must be a tricky way to steer, since all four motors had to furnish the same amount of thrust to keep the ferry moving in a straight line. Of course, those four sturdy boatmen had done all this before. They did it all day, every day, I told myself, looking at my watch. I realized I was biting my lower lip.

"Christ," said Maya. She was no sailor but even to her this looked like a shaky excuse for a boat. It occurred to me that she might be harboring some of the same problems with the starker aspects of reality that Bernard Emerson did. Not that I would ever suggest that to her.

One of the boatmen onboard raised his arm. If he was the captain, his uniform did not suggest that. It consisted of stained white painter's pants below a dark blue tee shirt advertising a well-known New York kosher deli. The lead car in the line drove on as far as the front end, at his gesture, keeping to the right. It was a white Toyota SUV. The next car boarded and lined up behind it. Then came a tour bus, pulling up to the front on the left alongside the two cars. This was a large luxurious Volvo coach that offered no space on either side for a person to pass on foot.

The ferry—I was now thinking of it as more of a barge—settled visibly in the water, disturbingly, as the bus came to a halt. I had the feeling we would soon be out of plumb on this crossing. The added weight of our Nissan could never offset the vast carcass of the tour bus. This platform was, after all, made completely of steel, which is not known to float on its own, even in an emergency. They had now loaded an entire bus full of people, thirty-five or forty trusting travelers (I tried not to think of them as stupid, but when you travel in a group you do take orders rather blindly), with all their gear onto the shoulders of these fragile drums of air under a welded sheet of quarter-inch steel. The papery skin of some of those barrels was probably rusted through by now after no one knew how many years of service. How much weight could they take before they gave up altogether with a subtle belch and simply sank to the bottom? Had some muddy scuba diver ever been under there with a powerful lamp to inspect them? Wasn't the nightly news always full of capsized ferry disasters in obscure third-world places throughout the world? And although we were not refugees fleeing the Sudan or Somali pirates, what place could be more obscure than this?

The scene reminded me of the opening footage of a disaster movie, where you can't quite conceive of what's coming but you know it's going to be terrible and there is no way in hell to stop it. All we lacked was the ominous background music.

Gradually I began to see this process as the aquatic version of the chicken bus system, but even more out of control. This ferry was probably owned by the same people, who even as we waited to board, were fingering stacks of greasy banknotes outside of some obscure bank vault in Guatemala City.

"Paul! Stop it, now!" Maya gripped my limp right hand. "Soon you'll start bleeding from the eyes." She did know how to read me.

The boatman waved to us cheerfully as he stepped off, as if he knew what was coming. I looked around, but there was no one behind us to yield to, so I drove aboard to fill the last space on the deck. From there, we'd never be able to reach the lifeboats in time, even if there had been any. A moment later we were rocking uneasily on the water. Cody and Maya both looked queasy. They weren't looking at me or at each other. I felt like if we capsized, that huge Volvo nightmare next to us would suck us all down with it into the muddy depths. Guatemala was a country that had an unfailing instinct to resist anything cutting edge in a heartbeat.

Each of the four outboard motors came to life with a gaggle of protesting coughs and tubercular sputters. As we crept away from shore my hands gripped the steering wheel like a lifebuoy, as if it could give us any control.

The breathless journey that followed took less than three minutes.

Once we were tied up on the wild shore beyond, the white Toyota came off first as if launched from a catapult. There were no buildings on that side of the Rio Pasión, and it streaked away on the road north. I could imagine the sense of liberation the driver was feeling. The next car ahead of us took its turn in a slightly less emotional way. Then the tour bus left at a still more dignified pace, and we followed with Maya biting her lip as she studied the map, searching, I'm sure, for a different route for our return.

"I would be quite happy to drive back through Honduras to avoid doing this again," Cody said. We all knew Honduras was the most dangerous country in the world that was not located in a war zone.

CHAPTER SIX

A t a few minutes before six P.M. we pulled into a tiny strip mall to pick up more bottled water, and more importantly, some additional quetzales. It held three shops, one of which was a convenience store with an ATM sign over the door. Although I knew we were close to our destination, the road offered nothing else but jungle for some distance in either direction on both sides, at least as far as we could see. Cody and I went in while Maya locked herself in the car. Without being a large establishment, the store offered ample supplies of wine, nuts, chips, and beer at prices about twice what we would pay at home in México. Next to the ATM stood a very bored and less than genial security guard wearing a black private agency uniform and a flak jacket, and carrying a black machine pistol. Why did his presence make me feel more at risk rather than less? His response to our greeting was at best no more than neutral. In the Agency we often tried to look formidable, but rarely larcenous, so his response seemed overdone.

I thought of the dense pedestrian traffic of Guatemala City, the shuffling kids slyly eyeing our pockets, our hands, wrists, and necks, the cutting edge athletic shoes of others, but where was the need for security like this, in the absolutely tropical vacancy of the central Petén? I reminded myself that I didn't understand how things went here, although I was getting more clues all the time.

"This place is just out of control," Cody said, shaking his head as he picked up a chilled six-pack of Moza Bock beer and set it on the counter. "For a convenience store that guy's got a lot of firepower in that MAC–10 he's carrying. Go ahead and use your debit card in that chancy machine and I'll hang back here ready for trouble."

His fingers subtly touched the shoulder holster under his left arm and he loosened the two top buttons of his shirt. Cody had done backup for both of us before, and from the look of the security guard, no one was going to mess with him either.

I coaxed the machine into giving me 2,000 quetzales, worth about $265 U.S. This was the most it would allow me, and it cost $10.80 in ATM fees, about ten times what it would've been at home in México for twice as much in pesos. Getting more quetzales than that would've required a second transaction. This was clearly an economy that was designed to clip the tourists. The guard wasn't watching me; he had looked away, possibly embarrassed at my victimhood. Once again I reminded myself that this was all on Bernard Emerson's tab. Now I understood more about his views of people and their cynical ways.

"Now I've got it. That guard is here to see that you are robbed only by the bank's ATM," I said to Cody as we paid for our snacks and wine, and left.

Sixteen kilometers up the road we came to earth at El Jardín de los Antiguos, The Garden of the Ancients, a name that may or may not have been reassuring. Maya had found this place online. She told us it was billed as thirty hectares (seventy-five acres) of natural lakeshore jungle, occupied by the same wildlife you would normally find there. Guests were requested to not disturb them, especially the crocodiles and the snakes. It was a logical jumping off place for Tikal, a little more than forty kilometers away to the north. But after our travels, we were not in a hurry to jump off for anywhere that evening.

Once we checked in and went down the curving path we saw that the lodgings were set up in a series of two-story clusters, each with two guestrooms per floor. These were laid out along a serpentine trail that bordered dense jungle. There was plenty of space between the buildings, and through the trees we caught glimpses of a substantial lake. The trees and vines advanced thickly to within a couple of meters of the walls.

As Maya and I stood on the small balcony of our room the birds greeted us as intruders. The trees were infinite in variety. I wondered how there could be so many different but successful solutions to evolving in that climate. The bark of each one was a study in test patterns of camouflage, a maze of lichen, mold, and fungus in subtle natural tones. I wanted to paint it. From the higher canopy a continual rain of leaves, twigs, bark fragments, and flower petals fell. Spattered with guano, this was a rich topsoil building by the hour. We were sitting on a tropical compost pit, an active caldron of organic decay and rebirth. No wonder biologists could come down here and discover unknown species. But what was Darren Hall discovering? Or perhaps his lunch with Theodore Asher meant nothing at all.

These residential buildings would probably have to be jacked up once each decade to maintain their position or they'd eventually be overgrown. Overhead the branches were filled with other forms of growth that had either landed there on a windy day or aggressively climbed into place, elbowing other competitors aside. It was surely not Eden, but it may have been the original melting pot of organic life. Eve wouldn't have needed an apple and a gullible companion to send this turbulent brew spiraling out of control.

We had barely unpacked when Cody pounded on the stout wooden door with his urban cop knock. "Now

I need a drink. Don't argue."

Maya took one of his huge hands in hers. "You were very brave today, darling."

Often her mouth is irresistibly sexy, and it was again as she said this.

Taking her cue, as he had so often before, he bent over so she could kiss his neck. Like me, and like most men, Cody could use some heartfelt support now and then. This is what I put up with to keep the Paul Zacher Agency the tightly knit team that it always is, mostly. The seductively reassuring nature of Maya Sanchez is definitely the glue that does it, some of the time. Don't ever think she doesn't know that, and as the head of the Zacher Agency her caress carries a special weight.

"We can open one of these wine bottles, or go to the real bar down the path," I suggested, wondering without saying so whether this intense organic stew around us might be offering a hint of something more sinister to come. It had a primitive, pre-human feel. Although at dusk it did not yet feel threatening, it was still much wilder than we were used to in the partly irrigated high desert plateau in the middle of México where we lived. There, the dominant plants were broccoli and cactus. We may have thought at home that we were living in Central America, but it was becoming clearer by the hour that there were widely different ways to define that term. Of course, as I recalled, by now Bernard

Emerson would be already on his way back to Panama. Had he tried to prepare us for this approaching tropical dislocation?

Just beyond the pool, the bar stood on the margin of a large complex that encompassed the restaurant, and on the approach side, the registration and service desk. From that position it would have caught the sunset for much of the year. What was most striking was how few walls were required to support or protect this. The restaurant was open on all sides except for the kitchen at the back and the rest rooms near the entry. The bar had a single rear wall for secure liquor storage, with a cooler and a freezer. I wondered why this food-filled space wouldn't be the headquarters for bugs big enough to cart the tables away? To rip large segments of skin from your neck as you ate? What was I missing here? The primitive woodsy scene around us was clearly out of control, yet somehow this rational oasis could still exist. Even though we in the Agency bill ourselves as detectives, you absolutely cannot figure out everything you're looking at. We settled at a table with a shore view and the waiter hurried over with menus for drinks and dinner. All of us sighed. It had been a very long day indeed. The perennial question was whether we'd been traveling toward the truth or away from it. You never knew the answer until the end, which was also when you learned whether you were going to get paid for this case.

After we ordered our drinks and deferred dinner, Cody pulled out his phone and punched in a number he'd drawn from his shirt pocket. He settled back in his protesting wicker chair like he'd been waiting for this moment. As it rang he whispered to us the words, "Theodore Asher," the guide from the lunch meeting with Darren at Chez Antoine in Panajachel, near the end of January.

Maya and I were content to let him take care of that business, so I took her hand. "You were always right about México," I said. "It's still the best place to be. I don't think this is."

"You're only looking at the trip today. But I told you as much when we met at that collage show at the Bellas Artes so long ago."

"You did. And I already knew that. What I didn't know yet that night was all there was to find out about you."

She lifted her glass to me. "And you still don't."

I felt her pulse; it was rising point by point.

Cody snapped his phone back into its belt sheath. The sound was a bit like a small book being slammed shut. "This is going to work. Asher has a client staying here that he needs to pick up for a tour of Tikal tomorrow, later in the day. But he says that's a magical time to be there, the best, in fact. I booked us a trio of tickets to go along with them. What I'm hoping is that the presence of this other person won't keep us from talking about Asher's meeting with Darren back in Panajachel."

"We can always be subtle," I said. No one responded.

"So," Maya said, "now we are simple tourists with a yen for ancient architecture. We will hook up with another naive soul staying in this resort and we will all share our insights. What does Theodore charge, by the way?"

"Fifty-five dollars apiece, and Asher does want it in dollars, plus the 150 quetzales to get in at the gate, so about seventy-five dollars each in total."

"All to be charged back to Bernard Emerson," Maya said cheerfully, always the accountant. After all, at the end of each case, she wrote the checks to settle the bills.

After a couple more rounds, we concluded that this cheery agency staff meeting had gone on longer than it would have at home in San Miguel, and under greater stress. I'm not sure whether the chief fueling agent was hope or relief, or merely the increasingly foreign setting. In any case, Maya and I tumbled into bed later ready for some further encounters on the edge of our normal decorum.

"This is what vacations are for," she said afterward. Without viewing it as a vacation myself, I did appreciate her point.

"And we have most of tomorrow off," I said. "I can handle that. We'll lie around the pool, take a few walks in the animal zones in our snake-proof shorts, and start fresh with Theodore Asher around 4:30. But I wonder whether he can add anything to this?"

"Darren Hall must have thought he might," said Maya.

CHAPTER SEVEN

Sometime during that night we were vocally assault-
ed by snores that could've come from a drunken
hippopotamus, or a covey of ancient Greek deities
revived in the sea. Deep, drawn out, and vibrating in a
timbre beyond human range or capability, they nearly
rattled the windows. Maya was never much of a snorer,
and when she did they were delicate and subtle. I moved
my ear closer to her face and heard nothing but soft and
peaceful breathing. The bedside clock read 5:13.

Another thundering snore, then another. Suddenly she sat bolt upright, gripping her bare shoulders
with both hands.

"Who is that?" I said, wishing I could sound reassuring. "If only we had that .45 now." I dropped my feet
over the side of the bed.

She shook her head and cleared her face. Normally she gathers her hair back and ties it loosely
before she goes to bed, but last night she hadn't thought
of it. "That only comes from howler monkeys. I knew I'd

heard it before."

"They must be huge."

"No, that's the whole group of them. It's their morning greeting. They can do it all at the same time."

"So they're welcoming the dawn in a chorus."

"I guess. Like dogs in a pack, is that the word?"

I fell back on the pillow with a groan.

After a while the serenade stopped, and we went back to sleep. But the rest we recovered was troubled and we were up with the sun less than an hour later. I made some coffee and we sat out on the balcony to listen to the birds awaken and sort out their preferences for the day. Understandably, their cries seemed emphatic and complaining.

Later we took a leisurely walk through the grounds. Aside from a sign about exercising some caution with the snakes, and not feeding the animals any packaged goods, little other guidance was offered. We saw only two fences. One enclosed the deer park, populated by dozens of small friendly critters that had adapted well to life on the grounds of a hotel. They studied the contents of our hands more than our kindly expressions.

The other chain link fence was somewhat different. About two meters high, it ran along the shore of the lake following a course five or six paces in from the water line. The purpose was not clear until we drew near the shoreline area below the bar and restaurant, terraced above us.

Like an armored but slightly tentative dark brown submarine, an enormous crocodile waited not three meters offshore; wallowing in the subtle blue eddies of the lake. In anticipation of breakfast, its head and upper back were defined by a series of knobby protuberances barely inching above the water. Six or seven turtles the size of a helmet paddled calmly around it as if waiting for scraps. Was the monster hoping we'd move just a bit closer? Did he even take the cyclone fence that seriously as a barrier? Because I no longer did. Or did the restaurant staff come out after serving breakfast to give him his normal diet of leftover omelets and cinnamon rolls, pork sausages and bacon? I could imagine them tossing it over the fence from a safer distance.

But was there any safe distance from that hungry fourteen-foot juggernaut? His single step was probably little short of a meter. This was a beast that was not coming over that fence, but why would going under it be any problem at all, with a two-foot snout like that, furnished with teeth like a buzz saw, to say nothing of a canny evil smile curling upward beneath his yellow gaze?

Those huge hypnotic catlike eyes engaged mine with a familiar scrutiny, that of predator and prey, until Maya yanked my arm. "It's time to eat or be eaten, Paul. Make your choice," she said. We turned and climbed the slope to the restaurant, frequently glancing over our shoulders. This is why she's the head of the Zacher Agency; she can always deliver common sense in a crisis.

After our late but substantial breakfast that morning Maya and I emerged to find the day's heat was already settling in thick layers over the Garden of the Ancients. Even that early in the day we suddenly felt overdressed. As an indicator of what was to come, six people were already either swimming or lounging around the pool. It was not quite ten o'clock. Perhaps the more benign angle of the sun at that early hour was the reason, but three women were lying face down on leveled deck chairs. One in particular caught my educated eye. She was a tall blonde in a turquoise bikini that suited both her skin tones and her contours quite well. As a painter, I have learned that harmony is good. One element should flatter another. Her hair was gathered in a bundle at the top of her head. Suddenly I realized how well I knew her, and how deeply we had connected in the past. I couldn't prevent myself from crying out in involuntary surprise.

"I swear that's Barbara Watt in the last chair!"

"What? What?" Maya said, scanning the group. "How do you know that?"

A tiny, but quite dangerous silence followed before I could respond.

"It's that..."

A cloud descended over Maya's face. "It's that you recognized her butt, isn't that it?"

"Yes, but not only that, of course. As you know, I have a near perfect visual memory. I painted her nude several years ago. Have you forgotten that?"

"Lucky you! How could I ever forget that for a single moment?"

Barbara may have heard this exchange, because she turned on one elbow and stared back at us. Her face took on a subtle smirk as she pulled her sunglasses down from the top of her head.

"Paul Zacher and Maya Sanchez. I guess we're all a very long way from home. It's been a while."

I had to think how long it had been. "It was during the Justus Barlow murder case when we last met, wasn't it? I believe you were harboring a suspect when we saw each other then." This was eight or nine cases back, one we had filed as *The Book Doctor*.

"That sounds like me." Getting to her feet, Barbara Watt pulled on a gauzy cover up and we moved to a table in the shade. "Of course, that woman was innocent."

I couldn't quibble with this. We had, after all, solved that case.

Maya was still studying her. "Are you on vacation?" she said finally in a tone that was meant to sound offhanded.

"More like a little business this time."

"I heard you've been out of the country lately," I said. This was no more than a surmise.

"Yes, although that was mostly in Peru. But as a collector, the Mayans are still my first love."

"I would've thought that was Paul," Maya said slyly. They shared a small, edgy but still marginally polite chuckle. I didn't join in. Barbara had been deeply involved in our first three cases as well as at the sidelines of the Barlow murder. When Maya left me for four months at the start of our fourth case, Barbara had taken me in after I was released from the hospital. In the days that followed she made some serious moves in my direction, and not for the first time, but I was too badly injured to take advantage of her offer. Images of that time were whirling past like a silent newsreel as I sat there. Suddenly I recalled the crocodile eyeing me two hours earlier.

"I suppose your collections must be enormous now," I said, heading for what I hoped was safer ground. My feet were already damp from the quicksand of this conversation.

"You wouldn't believe it. I don't know if you realize it, but there's a huge trade in looted antiquities here in Guatemala."

"I didn't know that, but I'm not surprised. None of the great Mayan cities have been more than fractionally excavated, and many of the lesser ones not at all, which creates a huge opportunity for looters. All they have to do is dig at the next mound."

"Beengo," said Maya, nodding supportively. "What are you looking for here, so close to Tikal?"

A waiter started to move toward us, but invisibly to the others, I waved him off with my hand below the seat of my chair. I didn't want any interruptions until we got more out of Barbara. I don't think she had an answer ready for Maya's question, because she studied her hands for a long moment. I couldn't help noticing that they were entirely free of any jewelry. After what we'd seen in Guatemala City, that was only prudent.

"Well, it's not a thing exactly that I'm looking for, but let me say this too. There have been times when I've taken a role in buying some contraband articles, not many, and not that much here in Guatemala before, but I believe people in my position, who have a bit of money to spend, can play an important role in seeing that some of the better looted items are protected by having them end up in good hands. People who understand what they're looking at. I think you both know that my collections will all go to the archaeological museum in Mexico City when I die. I view myself as a conservator in that way." She pulled the wrap back over her naked left shoulder. Having painted it in exquisite detail I knew her skin quite well. Artists don't forget, and of course, in many cases they don't try to. It's always helpful to remember what works.

"You don't think that buying contraband artifacts encourages looting?" said Maya sweetly, with a vague gesture that could've included the entire country. It was possible that looting had many meanings here.

Barbara shrugged. "Don't think I haven't considered that more than once. It goes on anyway, all over Central America, and if I were to drop out of the underground antiquities market nothing would change, except that more things would disappear into the wrong hands." "Still, I'm sure you'd be missed in some quarters," Maya said.

Then an idea hit me. Barbara had announced that she was not looking for an object, so it must be a person. Theodore Asher had told us he was coming late that afternoon because he already had a single passenger going to the ruins. He'd been eager to add three more from the Agency. I was sorting this out when Maya spoke again.

"You must be very excited about going to see the ruins this afternoon."

"Yes! You wouldn't believe how..." Even in the blooming heat, her face suddenly froze.

Stop, I said to Maya mentally, just stop right there. Scoring points on Barbara did not necessarily advance our mission, which had nothing to do with her, as I thought then.

"You're very quick," Barbara said. "How did you know that?"

"Because we're using Theodore Asher as a guide too," I said, "and he told us he already had one person to pick up here this afternoon. That it might be you was no more than a good guess. We're detectives, you know."

"Yes. I do know that. I've seen you in action."

Not as much as you would like, I thought. From the corner of my eye I saw Maya scanning my face, but I gave her nothing. I wasn't ready to ask Barbara whether she was looking for Darren Hall, but if she was, I wanted to discover that in a different context, because her search would've had a reason attached to it, one that might help us, and I didn't think she'd be ready to give it to us this early in the game. Being mostly naked in a public place, as she was, usually makes people talk less, not more. This time was no different.

"What do you know about Theodore Asher?" I said after a pause.

"I found him through some people I know who'd been to Tikal in the past. They called him Theo, and I think he prefers that. He's been a licensed guide for about fifteen years."

"You haven't met him yet?" Maya said.

"No, but I've also been told he can be a bit odd. Sort of spiritual, maybe you could call it; I don't know exactly. He started out as an archaeologist but later became caught up in this place in ways that went beyond the digs, and he never got away from it. He could never go *home* again. That happens. Some people get snared when they can feel the forces that are present here in ways that not everyone else can."

I wondered if this was what had also happened to Darren Hall.

Maya frowned as if she knew she wasn't going to relate much to Theo Asher.

I suppose I shouldn't have been surprised that Barbara was already connected in this way with a person we hadn't met either. Guatemala was not a large country, and for people with an interest in Mayan Mesoamerica, Tikal was the ultimate destination.

"What brought you here?" she said, more to Maya than to me. "I suppose you're working."

"Why would you think that?" I said.

"Because you're always working, Paul. I've never seen you on a vacation."

"You're right. Of course, just what we are doing here is confidential, as always." At that instant something occurred to me. It was a line that had first struck me from Bernard Emerson's opening letter: "*I learned about your services from one of your former clients. Although she asked me not to use her name, she told me she'd had a very positive experience with The Paul Zacher Agency...*"

Maya gave me a veiled look, as if she had

suddenly thought of this too.

"I wonder if you might have recommended us to our current employer?" she said.

Barbara gave her a puzzled look. "Can you give me a hint who that would be? Of course, I've always said your agency was the best in México. I've told that to a lot of people, but never to anyone down here."

"Bernard Emerson," Maya said.

"I'm sure I haven't ever heard that name before. Sorry." She looked away, not at anything in particular that I could see. It may have only been a way of not looking at us.

The conversation rambled on without revealing much more that could be of help. Ten minutes later I was careful to avert my gaze as Barbara Watt bent over, gathered up her things, and walked away. Maya and I made a point of not leaving at the same time she did.

"I can't say she's a welcome addition to our little group," Maya said two minutes later, looking off over the lake, her chin resting on her hand.

"I'm hoping she'll tell us who she's looking for and why."

"I know. That's why I fed her Bernard's name, trying to show some good faith."

"It didn't work."

"Not yet. Maybe later when she's had a chance to think about it more."

We spent the rest of the morning wandering over the property. A family of coatimundi began to follow us, doglike creatures with acutely pointed noses and ringed tails. They were serious and fearless in approaching us without being exactly friendly. The babies scrambled ahead of us and climbed trees to the height of our hands, highly focused and sniffing the air carefully. I've heard that we also have them in San Miguel, but I've never seen any there. Finally they gave up on us and wandered off. The park was endlessly foreign and exotic, but now we were too distracted to appreciate it.

Maya was still a little tense during a late lunch and afterward we read outside on our tiny terrace among the restless treetops. On my laptop I went back into the files and reviewed Bernard Emerson's notes on his inquiries, but found little more to help us. He hadn't identified Theo Asher as a possible connection with Darren Hall, and so he hadn't talked to him. There was no sign Emerson had ever come up to Tikal. My overall sense was that he had lacked follow through, perhaps thinking that he could hire it from us, as he had.

At 4:30 we all met in front of the reception area. We hadn't run into Cody earlier, so he was greatly surprised to see Barbara Watt waiting with us when he came up the path. Involuntarily his hand brushed his shoulder holster hidden under the broad outlines of the tropical shirt.

TWILIGHT AT TIKAL

As we waited for our ride to the ancient city I still could not believe there was no connection between Barbara Watt and Bernard Emerson.

CHAPTER EIGHT

Theo Asher did not arrive driving a chicken bus. We were relieved to see him pull up in a white eight or ten-year-old Chevrolet passenger van with eight seats and ample luggage space. It had been immaculately kept up.

Our guide was tall and lean with bronzed arms and face, wearing a sun faded floral print cotton shirt and newish khaki pants with extra pockets. His sensible hat reminded me of the one Bernard Emerson had worn in Guatemala City. Theo's mobile face and wide expressive mouth were welcoming to each of us in turn. He paid no special attention to Barbara, although she could cause many men to stutter.

Once we were aboard he sketched out our visit as we drove toward the exit. We would be at the gate of the national park that sheltered Tikal in twenty-five minutes. The ticket stop was in an area that also offered restrooms with a restaurant and gift shop. From there it was about twelve minutes more to the edge of the ruins inside the park. If we all did not have a water bottle, mosquito protection, and a serviceable hat we could get them there. But in fact we were all ready.

Once we crossed the gate and paid our entry tolls, the park interior looked much like the exterior. The jungle appeared thick and complex, as if any variety of vegetation could make it there, although I saw no pine trees or ordinary hardwoods like we had in Ohio. I did pick out a few mahoganies, whose look I knew from my woodworking days. All the while I had the sense we were being watched by creatures big and small as we drove through.

"The trees have eyes," I said to Maya. She folded her arms and looked away. Once in the Yucatán Cody had sliced a falling coral snake in half with his machete as it tried to drop around her neck.

"You are living in Flores?" Cody said, seated behind Theo.

"Yes, the local people call it the gateway to Tikal. It's no more than a tourist town on the water, I suppose, but I can get by reasonably enough there. It's a little cooler at night since it faces Lake Petén Itzá. At this altitude, you know, it's pretty warm year round."

"What is the altitude here?" Barbara said.

"Just a little over a hundred meters. I think the Mayans preferred that, although there's a whole different group of mountain Mayans in Chiapas. But the Yucatán is pretty low too."

"I don't suppose you get down to Lake Atitlán very much," I said, trying to sound like I always sought out lakes whenever I traveled.

"No, that's kind of far off my beat, although I was down there in Panajachel a little more than three months ago to pick up a group of Germans that wanted to see Tikal. There were eight of them, so it was worth my while to make the trip."

"They *made* it worth your while," Barbara said.

"Yes, and they paid in cash with dollars, which are very easy to use here. They're actually better than quetzales. Besides, I had learned a good bit of German in college, enough to read Schliemann's reports in the original. That helped too."

"Schliemann?" Barbara said.

"Heinrich Schliemann discovered the ruins of Troy in the 1870s."

"Those must've been the great days of archaeology," Barbara said, "with discoveries like that waiting to be made."

As if that was our cue, we pulled up to the edge of a clearing and stopped. No one else was in view, either on foot or in a vehicle, but I could imagine that most people preferred to visit in the cool of the morning. As we emerged from the long, scattered shadows of the trees the immense backside of a Mayan temple pyramid confronted us. It had to be fifteen stories high or more. Waves of absorbed heat came off it. This rear view offered little detail beyond the dark crusty texture of the stone. Then, at the top, a ruined comb, as they called it, a finishing decorative touch crowning the white blockhouse at the pinnacle. This, I thought, was probably not the way most Mayans had approached this place fifteen hundred or two thousand years ago.

Theo turned to face the four of us as we stopped at the base. He seemed about to deliver a prepared speech. I suppose his statements all must be prepared after doing this for as long as he had.

"By now you will have examined the site map I gave you when we started out. We are standing on the south side of a great public square, the most sacred one in this city, and the oldest. This temple behind me is faced by another similar one directly across the plaza, but that one is even somewhat larger. On the right, once we come around to the front of it, is a much lower mausoleum complex for the burial of nine nobles and three lesser kings and queens. Immediately on our left you will see the ball court, and above and behind it, the viewing stand for the ruler and his friends and family. Imagine yourself as a visitor here in the year 300, when this place still had 500 plus years of glory ahead of it. We are only trying to fit in, if a little late. Any questions so far?"

All of us were ready to proceed, but we had no

more questions at that point. Barbara snapped a few shots with her cell phone.

"OK then." Theo took half a dozen more steps and turned again. "I want to add that for me, for reasons both personal and historical, this is a sacred place. We are no more than time travelers here, interlopers walking in from a century unthought-of by the people who built and inhabited this place, those who flourished here. When this city was abandoned not long after the year 800, when this branch of Mayan culture had run its course after fifteen hundred years, Charlemagne was the new ruler in Europe. He was the *future*, to the Europeans, but to the Mayans in this city he would've been an upstart of no importance."

I know a bit about history, and although this was an intimate perspective, I was gaining in respect for Theo Asher. In the heartfelt delivery of his presentation it was also easier now to think of him as Theo rather than Theodore.

Silence, or was it awe, overcame us in the center of the square framed by those monuments. Standing in places like that I could never prevent myself from thinking of all the people that had stood there before me. What had they seen? The parades, the ceremonies, the executions and sacrifices with severed heads bouncing down eighteen or twenty stories of steps. For today's reality, the coarse tropical grass we stood on had been mowed and trimmed like a golf green. I had to wonder about the texture of it then. Maybe it was more about control now. In the Yucatán they had told us that if you did not keep the pyramids cleared of vegetation, they would be entirely covered over again in only 100 years.

"We are here at a special time of day," Theo continued in a lower tone of voice. "Some of you might think this is too late in the afternoon to visit this place. Maybe you thought the heat would be overwhelming."

"Special time of day for us or for the ancients?" Maya said. She was in her native mode now, where no gringo was going to tell her what was doable or appropriate in Latin America.

Theo turned to her. "You will experience it if you are able to. Being open to it will help. Come with me."

She turned up her nose at this. Behind the ball court, from which, I noticed, the target circle was missing from its normal spot high on the side wall, we followed Theo up a roughly restored range of steps. It was more than two stories but less than three. The Mayan perspective on step design would've been banned by OSHA. Each step was about seven inches deep on the tread and thirteen inches high on the riser. It made going up seem an off-balance stretch, but from the top, when you turned around to look down, you realized that the ascent had been the easiest part. I had observed this before on a trip to Uxmal, in the Yucatán, before I'd met Maya.

111

From this perspective the group burial of lesser nobility and royalty across the plaza made more sense. Whatever had once sheltered the executive seats on this side was now collapsed and cleared. What remained looked more like unrestored bleachers.

At the top, Barbara surprisingly moved in and took Theo's hand as we sat down on a row of carved blocks. Her voice was soft and intimate as she drew him closely beside her. She continued to hold his hand as she spoke.

"I can feel that something important happened to you here. Am I right that it was a milestone in your life?"

At the pool she had told us she was not on vacation. I now began to see Theo as part of her job, her mission.

After a pause that may have come either from surprise or pain, Theo said, "Her name was Saskia." I could see that he was not going to be any match for Barbara. "She was a Dutch student doing a year at Brown after starting in archaeology at home at Leiden University. Like me, she wanted an advanced degree, but most of their studies in Europe are focused in Asia and the Middle East. The program there is excellent, but Saskia had a special love for the indigenous people of Central America. She and her family had traveled in Guatemala when she was a child, and this is where she needed to work."

"I suppose she took your class when she got to Brown," Maya said softly. Her look was encouraging, as if she had caught Barbara's lead, although that would've been a first.

Theo shrugged as he shifted about on the ancient stones searching for a more comfortable position. "Yes, but my class was only about procedures, three credits of the most basic stuff. You had to know it before they would release you onto even the most picked-over archaeological site, and even though she'd had a similar course at Leiden, they insisted she take mine too. It was about how to dig, how to handle and preserve artifacts, how to protect the site as you exposed different layers to the elements, and how not to contaminate things yourself. They had their own procedures. Before long I could see that Saskia was a natural. She had an instinctive grasp of the process. I was only a first year instructor."

"But they still sent you down here?" I said. This didn't seem likely or right.

"No, not Brown. I was too far down the seniority list to merit anything like that. But a foundation with an independent program for Guatemala sites put up a flyer in our department office. Among their offerings they had a one-time grant funded by some millionaire hobbyist and they announced it right after Christmas. Thinking nothing would happen, Saskia and I both signed up. We were both chosen."

"Were you already lovers by that time?" Cody said. His narrowed eyes probed the empty plaza below. Theo took no offense at this direct question as he nodded. "After that we were the only ones for each other, ever."

"Then you and Saskia must have loved it here," Maya said.

Theo nodded sadly. "Even to the extent that we didn't go back with the other seven when the field trip was finished that winter. Of course you couldn't work here in the summer."

"Why was that?" Cody said. His tiny notebook had appeared in his hand, although I hadn't seen it emerge from his pocket.

"You just wouldn't believe the heat. It's still early May now and the traffic here has already fallen off sharply." Here Theo paused to look again at the cluster of mausoleums across the plaza, a space that had been abandoned for more than twelve hundred years. I wondered whether he was now sitting in the exact seat of the ruler, or of ten of them in a series. "I am not a New Age kind of person, so don't think that's why I'm going to say this, OK?"

"Why then?" Barbara said.

"Saskia and I had found that this was our place, as if we owned it. It had been a powerful enough site for the Maya to build this incredible city twenty-five hundred years ago. Why couldn't we rediscover some of that same power? You only had to see it as they did, to feel it. I can feel it now." He rubbed his thumb across the tips of his other fingers to savor the texture of it.

"You and Saskia must have found a way to recover it for yourselves," Maya said. I gave her a quizzical look, but she was already launched on her own path.

"We did. Once we were on our own here we formed a team to guide tourists through the ruins. We knew things about Tikal that the guidebooks didn't reveal. People were thrilled to speak with real archaeologists who had actually worked this site. But then four and a half years after we both left the project to stay here together, Saskia died of ovarian cancer. She was hoping to reach her thirtieth birthday, but she didn't quite make it.

The violent exhale of breath from Maya seemed to underline this. "How terrible! But what about the health care here?"

"Yes, it was very good, but when the tumor was discovered, it was too late to keep it from going all through her."

"But still you stayed on at Tikal after she was gone," Barbara said. "Wasn't that painful?"

Theo raised his eyebrows in a tolerant look. "No, it was reassuring, and it sustained me rather than torturing me. I stayed on because she was still here. I would never leave Saskia."

This statement was met with silence. After a moment Maya cut through it. "Where is Saskia now?"

Theo rose, his thin native shirt rippling in the soft breeze, and extended both arms toward the central plaza below. "What you are seeing here beyond the ball court is the main necropolis of Tikal. Some of the great rulers are still sleeping here deep within the stones."

"Are you suggesting that not all these pyramids have been excavated?" said Cody, clearly trying to tame the normally gruff tone of his voice. Dusk was gathering around the scene, thickening the shadows.

"The first one was, on the right where we came in, but in the second one here on the left they have never found the burial. The king is still there, of course, waiting. And there are others not far away that still withhold their secrets."

Waiting for what? I thought. Certainly not for being dug up to be displayed in a museum while tourists shoot the scene with their cell phones, or turn and snap selfies backed by the royal bones.

"Saskia has joined them somehow," Maya said. "Is that what you're telling us?"

Theo sat down again on the weathered carved stone.

"As her health failed we sketched this all out. She

was very brave, very rational, more so than I was. That was her style. Her parents were both killed in a car accident in Belgium when she was twenty-one. She had no siblings so she left her money to me, knowing I would use it to stay here. Some of it went for that passenger van, but I still have the greatest part of it. Most days I can easily make a living as a guide. Some people tip well. That's all I want for myself now."

I wasn't sure whether this was a high calling or a compromise more like treading water. "How did you manage to have her buried here? Why would they allow that?" I said. "This is a national park."

Theo shook his head and remained silent for a moment, studying the court below.

"No, I knew they wouldn't allow it, so I didn't ask permission to do what I did. Saskia isn't buried at all. She wanted to be cremated. Every day for about a month afterward I came out here early and took a bag of her ashes with me in my pocket. I scattered them around all the buildings, tracing back and forth among them in a mystical maze I designed myself. It's partly based on the Mayan calendar. I have a pass as a licensed guide, so I can come and go here freely any time. For a while they were giving sound and light shows, so I was here a lot in the evening. His arm took in the entire site with a broad sweep. His smile suggested he'd achieved his life's goal. "Now Saskia is everywhere, all around us. Can't you feel her presence?"

An awkward silence followed as none of us responded.

"And is this sunset hour special to her, or to you?" Barbara said finally. The light was now palpably starting to fail. Soon there would be bats swooping down to get snagged in our hair, I thought. Maya detests bats.

"They'll be coming very soon," Theo said slowly in an almost ceremonial tone, folding his hands and placing his elbows on his knees. "The spirits of the ancients come to dance at this hour. Saskia is one of them now. I can only be thankful for that, and I know that was her desire. We spoke of it at the end."

Cody gave me a queasy look. New Age material was not his favorite territory. Maya shifted uneasily, leaning against my shoulder. The setting was spooky enough even in full steamy daylight, with its monstrous crumbly towers, several taller than a twenty-story building, its inerasable aura of death and abandonment, the former glory of a great people reduced to relics by the centuries-long ravages of time. Did the forgotten godlike rulers linger on in spirit, some of them even still here physically, now only bones among their burnished jade ornaments? Tikal had once been the most impressive city in the Americas, many centuries before these continents were even thought of as the Americas.

"So, where will they be coming from?" Cody said

softly. "When they do come tonight." Not if they come, I thought.

"You saw the three reservoirs on the left as we drove in. That was where the ancients quarried the limestone to build this city, and in the deep hollows that were left behind, their water supply collected as the rain fell. As with so many other things, they were very clever about that. Over time, like everything else here, they soon became filled with soil and vegetation once they were no longer maintained. That is also where our friends will come from, very soon now."

"Very soon now," Barbara repeated. Her eyes rested on my face. In this place I had no answers for her, just as I'd had none when she was chasing me around the studio when I was painting her on our first case. No one ever wants the answers that come too easily.

As I was trying not to imagine what these approaching creatures might look like, pushing away thoughts of the Black Lagoon, three fireflies emerged from nowhere and flashed past our faces, spiraling round each other. Theo gave a small welcoming chuckle.

"Saskia is welcoming you now," Theo said with a broad grin that was growing more vague in this light. "She is with her friends."

"Those would be some of the past rulers of this place?" Cody said, trying to sound liberal and open minded.

"Only on sacred ceremonial occasions. But the dead of this holiest of places all live on as fireflies, *las luciérnagas*, so Saskia has now returned with the artisans, the potters and the stonecutters, the women who cooked and cared for the young and the old, who dressed the dead for burial as this place faded into history. She is now with those who danced in the great square below us, and especially, those who carved and polished the sacred jade. That's what she wanted for her eternity, to be one of those workers, not a deity, of course, but a common person who was part of an ageless sacred tradition. One that will last forever."

"And will you join them too one day?" Maya said softly. Normally she avoided anything to do with religion. Maybe what we were hearing wasn't even what she thought of as religion.

"That is always my hope. That's why I cannot ever leave this place."

At that moment, as if in an affirmative response, thirty or forty more fireflies converged and flickered around us. I felt all of us relaxing as we watched them dance their evening ceremony. It seemed like quite a while before any of us spoke again but I couldn't have said how long it was. Time didn't matter here now, and it hadn't in ages.

"This is a wonderful and very spiritual occasion," Maya said in a sympathetic tone. "What did Darren Hall think when you brought him here to see it? Was this especially what he came to see?"

She had chosen this moment to get to the heart of our visit. Barbara hadn't expected this and I think in that faded light her eyes narrowed suddenly, although I wasn't sure. If Theo's reaction was consternation, he was quicker to conceal it than I was to observe it. Of course the light on his face was no longer what it had been, either.

"So you know Darren?" Theo said.

"We are acquainted with his uncle much better than with him," I said. "That's how we knew Darren came here." Below us, as shadows clotted further beyond the base of all the ruins, the fireflies developed into a lacy light source, the strongest that remained.

"Darren left us a message at our hotel in Panajachel on an earlier trip," Cody said. "That's why we came here. It told us that he was looking for something. I don't remember the exact words anymore, and he may not have said what it was in any detail, other than that he planned to meet you up here in the Petén. Now I wish we had kept it. I guess that at first it didn't seem important. He was mainly a guy we knew of, more than one we knew personally. I mainly remember that curly red beard."

In the uncertain twilight flicker of the fireflies, Theo's face grew more serious. "He did come up here on the same small bus as the German tourist group. I couldn't fit them all in my van so I rented it. No matter if you lost that message, I can at least tell you what I told him, but it's better if I show you. I'm glad now that I brought my torch. Normally I'd be starting on my way back about this time before darkness falls completely. The darkness here is more intense than anywhere I've ever been."

"No problem, I always carry one with me too," Cody said.

Theo led us up the eroded stairs past the back of what he had called the executive viewing stand. It ended in a wall about a meter and a half high, and beyond it the overgrown rubble signaled the edge of the city, or at least of the excavated part.

"From where we are standing now there is still a large part of Tikal ahead of us," Theo said. "It's only been about fifteen percent excavated, but it's all been mapped from the air."

"What are they waiting for to finish?" said Barbara.

"Money. There are no monuments of this size left in the city to impress the tourists. Not that there aren't some important finds for archaeologists still to be made." About ten meters further the ground fell away into a shallow gully. We slipped through the weedy growth down to that level and Theo stopped before a sloped stone-framed entrance that was sealed by a pair of locked steel doors. Cody scanned the surface with his small lamp. It was smooth and modern, painted forest green.

Theo turned to face us. "Two of the temple burials that were discovered below displayed a peculiar feature. One was from Burial 48, the grave of Siyaj Chan K'awil from the year 457, and the other was Burial 85 from the early first century of this era, Great Jaguar Paw, the ninth ruler of Tikal. They were normal in almost every way, with several servant sacrifices to wait on the deceased king in the afterlife, and quantities of pottery and jade ornaments. But the heads and the long thighbones—the femurs, if you will, of those two kings were missing."

"I don't understand that," I said. "Why dismember the corpse of the ruler?"

"Neither did we, until we discovered this enclosure where we're standing tonight." He placed his palm on the sloped doorframe. "Our mission with that research grant was to sensitively probe the edges of the established digs. You see, this find you're looking at here was the climax of my expedition with Saskia. This opening was then faced with a stone slab that was totally overgrown and fractured in the middle. No carving or other information was on it. I wish I could take you inside and show you what we found, but I was recently caught in a small indiscretion, and I don't have access to it anymore."

"What was that indiscretion?" said Barbara. This was a key word to her. I couldn't think of anyone who had a greater mastery of the subject, and she was always ready to add more nuance to her command of it.

"I would never bring people up here, but Darren Hall wanted to see the interior in the worst way. I could still come and go freely from the guardhouse at the gate, so for a small gratuity over my normal fee I borrowed the key that afternoon and I let him in. Frankly, I didn't see any harm in it, since the contents had already been cleared years before. Saskia and I had even helped to do it. Now it's not much to look at."

"And?" said Cody, leaning toward him in a persuasive way. At six-foot-three, anytime he leaned over someone it felt persuasive.

"When I returned the key later someone had noticed it was missing and since then I've been barred from that secured store room at the entrance to the park."

"¡*Que lástima!*" said Maya, softly. "What a shame!"

"I'm sure, but it will be far from a total loss tonight," Cody said as he reached into his left pants pocket and pulled out his lock picks. "Hold onto this, Paul." He handed me his small torch to light his effort as he got to work on the lock.

A Mayan lock, whatever that might have been, would've been tougher to get through. This one was a normal piece of American consumer hardware of no extraordinary complexity. You would've seen it in the States as a routine installation on the side door of anyone's suburban garage. Fifty seconds later Cody threw back the door with a small grunt. Two flashlight beams probed the interior.

"So it's a peasant burial?" said Barbara, peering into the chamber without advancing. As a collector of legendary antiquities this sounded like a major disappointment for her.

The room was narrow under a corbelled ceiling, the kind that tapers upward row by row toward a peak. It offered four bare human-sized stone slabs lying in a row, and nothing else. There was about a meter of space between each of them and another meter between the foot of each and the right side wall. No decoration or Mayan script had been used. At the back wall toward the square below there was a hollow in the floor that was probably a drain to siphon off any seepage from outside.

"I know it looks like nothing now," Theo said. "But when we first opened this room three of these slabs each had a skull and two thighbones. The skulls were covered with the most elaborate jade death masks I have ever seen. They were high royalty."

"And what did Darren Hall say when he saw this cleared space?" Maya said. "Wasn't it the whole point of his visit?"

"He was surprised, and then almost ecstatic. I told him that for a long time we didn't understand why the royal skeletons had been divided like this. It was only seven years later that our team leader, Professor Engebretson, came up with a plausible answer."

"And that was?" said Barbara, in the rising tone of one asking for the name of the winner at the Oscars.

"You can probably figure this out too. The Mayans were always at war among themselves. It was a way of testing the prowess of their individual city, and of dominating and controlling the limited resources around them. It was more than a hobby, it was a career, and it was not about principle or ideology. It was merely competition."

"I can imagine that sometimes one side won a round, and then the other side did," said Cody.

Theo nodded rapidly. "Right, and often on the losing side the king was killed in battle. In fact, that may have defined the losing side. Battle was always a test for the kings, since they couldn't nominate anyone else to lead the forces in their place. That could constantly be a tipping point."

"But still," said Maya, "why divide the bodies?"

"It was a long tradition that concerned mobility, the ability of the tribe to expand at its neighbor's expense. When the king's side lost and he was captured, he was executed and his head and thighs were preserved as trophies by the winning side. But because they were so important and symbolic of victory, they were always displayed in a place of honor in the winners' capital city."

I was starting to see this better now. "And so when they fought again, if the side that had earlier been defeated won in the return contest, they could recover all those trophies of their former leaders. The partial dead, the sacred relics of their kings."

"Yes!" Theo said. "And this place where we are standing tonight was where they put them."

"But it's not very fancy for royalty, is it?" said Barbara. Interior design mattered deeply to her in her great Los Balcones neocolonial mansion in San Miguel.

"Right, and that's part of the explanation. They could not disturb the previous partial burials in these elaborate temples to unite them with the rest of their remains, because the Mayans had a heavy taboo about doing that. Taboos involving royalty are the harshest ones. So they simply placed the recovered body parts honorably, if somewhat minimally, here."

"In a place where they could overlook the ball court as in life," I said.

"And they were just lacking one more set of recovered skull and femurs to fill in that bare slab at the end of the row," said Maya.

The radiating glow from Cody's torch illuminated an uncomfortable look on Theo's face.

"I guess you could say that. But when we opened this crypt, it was not the final slab in the row of four that was unoccupied, it was the third one." He walked in further and placed both palms on it. "This one was empty."

"How did you react to that?" I said, thinking that it meant something I didn't understand.

"Our project leader wrote later that there must have been one more in the sequence of rulers whose body parts they were hoping to recover, and they had left an opening for him in the order that he had ruled. Those remains must've been held by a tribe they hadn't met in battle for a while, and they never did again before Tikal fell into ruins."

"And," Maya said, "how did Darren Hall react when you told him that?"

Lit from the two uncertain hand torches below, Theo's face was distorted by unlikely shadows. The bottom of his nose and the underside of his lower lip and chin were the brightest parts of his face. We all must have looked much the same. "It was the oddest thing. 'You're sure it was the second from the last in that row?' he asked me. I said again that it was, and I repeated that I had been here at the opening, from the moment when the stone covering was first removed. This burial had been sealed until then. 'Has this account been published in the journals?' he added after a while. I said that it had. I even gave him the reference, since I still remembered it, and that was all. I relocked the door and we went back to the gate. He was very quiet. The German tourists had watched this in silence, mostly."

"Did Darren say where he planned to go next?" Cody said.

"No, only that he had a lot of work to do. But then, you know, he was an anthropologist, and I've never had a good handle on how they think. I always thought he might have seen something in the way those remains changed hands back and forth. But, you know for an archaeologist like me, it's usually based much more on the physical evidence. Don't tell me about their feelings for each other; I want to see the artifacts they left behind and what they thought those artifacts did for them."

"Did he say whether he was married?" Barbara asked. I didn't see how this fit in.

"He had a fiancée that he mentioned several times, and he said her name was Ixobel, I think. That's all the personal detail I know about him. Two days later I hired a local driver to take them all back to Panajachel and turn in the bus, and I resumed my normal guide duties."

"And that driver would've taken a chicken bus back to Flores," I said.

"Of course," Theo said in a tone that suggested there was no other option.

When Theo dropped us off at The Garden of the

Ancients, Barbara gave him a substantial tip, saying it was from all of us.

"Don't be fooled," Maya said to no one in particular as we walked away.

CHAPTER NINE

At the first hint of dawn the howler monkeys again came at us with their grotesque symphonic snores. In the treetops the birds began bickering about the coming day's program, and below us on the jungle floor something uniquely ponderous or even prehistoric shuffled through, concealed beneath the dimly lit canopy of the undergrowth. We never did see what it was, but it was clearly big enough to not be concerned about stealth. Had we come to earth on the set from *Jurassic Park*? No, it was just another promising morning being launched in the Garden of the Ancients.

Maya and I found each other beneath the sheets—no blankets had been required—and curled up together. After we'd parted from Barbara in the driveway the previous evening we hadn't seen her again. She may have had dinner in her own room, but that didn't mean we had overlooked her reaction to the name of Darren Hall. We were both ready to reconsider the issue of what she might be up to.

On the evening before, the Paul Zacher Agency had met in executive session in the open-air restaurant over dinner without her. The building—I wanted to think of it as a tropical lodge—was a remarkable blend of construction styles, with a wide variety of peeled logs anchored into steel brackets mounted on posts. This structure supported a high thatched roof with some degree of authority.

"I'm having the pork," Cody said. "I've heard that pigs do well in this climate. I'm not sure I can say that about myself." Wide irregular patches of sweat reached down his sides.

"I'll have the shrimp brochette with saffron rice and a glass or two of the Chilean Chardonnay," said Maya. Her broad smile was directed at both of us. Wondering if they catered to a strong following among German tourists, I ordered the schnitzel.

"Let's talk about Barbara," Maya said after the drinks arrived, putting on a cheerful face. "What is she really doing here?"

"I think she's doing the same thing we are," Cody said. "Looking for Darren Hall, and for the same reason, only she probably knows better than we do what that is."

"You mean we aren't only trying to put our hand on Darren's shoulder and when we do, we turn his whereabouts over to Uncle Bernie?" I said. "She's gotten into this venture with more depth than we have, I'm afraid."

"She has deeper pockets than Bernard Emerson," Maya said.

"It's just this." Cody leaned forward. "When somebody hires me to find a person, and I discover that person is looking for an unknown thing, then I have to wonder whether the person that hired me is really looking for that thing too."

"So if Barbara is in that same queue," I said, "is she also looking for that thing too, more than Darren is? Then why don't we simply ask her that directly?"

"And get some phony answer," Maya said, flatly.

"Then we'll draw her out. I'm sure we'll see her in the morning."

We spent the rest of that evening talking about Theo and his strange obsession with Tikal and the departed but still ever-present Saskia. By so consciously embedding her ashen remains in that ancient city, even using a maze of his own devising, he had locked himself in place there too. It made me wonder whether some of us design and construct our own prisons, whether as a reward, or even as a punishment.

By the time we parted that evening it was clear to all of us that our next stop would have to be the colonial city of Antigua. Our focus would be the address that Bernard Emerson had given us as the last contact information for Darren Hall. We had tried to reach him every day, but he was still not answering his email or phone calls. Maya sent a brief progress report to Bernard Emerson, one that offered little detail, which is exactly as much as we knew. The woeful tale of Theo and Saskia certainly would've given it more texture, but that was almost all we had. In his encouraging response he offered no more information than he had originally.

When we reconvened for breakfast at about eight o'clock the next morning, Barbara was already seated in the restaurant ahead of us, looking fresh and put together for a road trip that might end up in the jungle. She wore a trimly fitted safari shirt in a pale khaki tone, darker khaki slacks, hiking boots, and at her collar a slender knotted silk neckerchief in red orange that perfectly accented both the outfit and her blue eyes. Again, she had no jewelry. With only a few of her more impressive diamonds, which I knew she owned, she might have fit in well on Rodeo Drive in Beverly Hills.

"Good mornin', y'all." Barbara Watt had never lost her Birmingham, Alabama accent, even if it still had a slight Texas overlay from living in Dallas for five years with her late husband, Perry. In front of her were coffee, fresh squeezed orange juice, and a plate of mango, pineapple, kiwi, and banana chunks from the buffet.

"I need bacon," said Cody, "and some eggs. Mangoes never took me anywhere when I was on the force in Peoria."

"Mangoes never even reached you in Peoria," Maya said.

"Bring me a hardboiled egg when you come back then, would you, Cody darlin'?" Barbara said. "Ones with a brown shell, not white. I do need some protein, but I don't care for anything bleached."

Maya's eyes narrowed at this sudden familiarity with our business partner, one whose affections she wore like a logo tee shirt from Woodstock. But in the past we had all survived some tight situations together. Her experience prompted her to always be looking for new ways to push Barbara away. I could understand that too. As Maya and Cody headed for the buffet table I sat down across from Barbara with a frank look. I do this expression well, since it's so useful with suspects.

"While I am rarely surprised to see you turn up in my life, even here in Guatemala, I'm still sometimes at a loss to know why that happens. Help me out here. What are you up to? We're family, or we would be if you'd snared me one of those many times you tried. Out here in the jungle, you don't have to play things so close to your vest."

She gave me her most seductive smile; one I don't think Cody or Maya had ever seen, but I could've painted it from memory, even as a billboard. "This far down the road in the jungle, isn't that what you mean, Paul? It's about our history, yours and mine."

"Well, yes. We can learn more from history than most people like to think."

Again she glanced toward the buffet, where Maya and Cody were lifting the lids to pass each dish in review, voting it up or down. "If I answer you frankly, then you might have to regard me in a different way."

"Of course. Now you've become Florence Nightingale. That's good, since I can show you the scars from our previous encounters. Maybe you can prescribe a salve."

She only grinned and picked delicately at her fruit. "I'm sure you must think you're making a joke about us."

"Maybe. Just give me the truth. I'm already on duty today and I get paid by the hour."

"All right, I'll let you in on a secret. I came here to find Darren Hall." She turned to look me straight in the eye.

"I can believe that. But why does he need to be found? Isn't he a grownup?"

"He's been kidnapped."

Looking around to check that I wasn't still in Guatemala City, I knew I could buy into that idea too, and it hardly even took me by surprise. Not that I had any facts to support it, but the atmosphere, the surroundings, the mood, even the goddam wallpaper in this country reeked of it, not that they used wallpaper for anything more than to cover over the facts of what was going on.

"Tell me more, starting with how you know that, or at least, why you think you know it."

Barbara slowly shook her head. "I can't tell you any more."

"Why not? Aren't we in this together now?"

"This is a highly confidential situation," she said, leaning over the table with her shoulders drawn slightly together. "This is a game where not everyone gets to play, do you know what I mean? Not that you don't believe you're in it already. But thinking you're a part of something this big isn't enough. This is a game that has levels and levels. You may think Theo knew something last night, but he doesn't. He's using Tikal like a narcotic, to get him through life, but he's not learning anything from it anymore. He's too inward, he's only self-absorbed, which is not enough to win this game. I only went out there yesterday to see whether he knows as much as I do. He doesn't, trust me on that."

This made me reach back into my darkest experience of Barbara Watt, unfulfilling as it had been. A single glance told me that Maya and Cody were progressing to the end of the offerings at the buffet, where they were now scanning the waffles. I could imagine that Cody was commenting on the syrup. Only real maple would do. Time was running out and I needed to say something to either move this on or wrap it up. Perhaps if I reminded her of our former closeness I could get more out of her. I leaned sharply over the table.

"It's in times like this that I wish I had fucked your brains out on one of the twenty-six different occasions you offered me that option."

Unimpressed by this, her eyebrows went up delicately. "You really counted that many, Paul? Was each refusal like a tiny merit badge on your sleeve? Maya must've enjoyed sewing them on. I'm sure she has a very fine hand."

I was suddenly reminded that while Guatemala was full of crooks with a wide variety of motives, not all of them were amateurs. "No, that count is only a rough guess. It could be more."

"Well, I wish you had taken me up on at least one or two of them, possibly five or more, but that wouldn't help you today. Anyway, I quickly get bored with any game with no outcome. What we have here on this occasion is the money shot, Paul. This is the big one. It's a shame you didn't make the cut on one of your earlier tries."

Possibly. "How big? Tell me!" I placed my hand on her wrist, wondering whose failure it had really been. In the tiny silence that followed I sensed she was gathering her files into headlines. This might be the breakthrough we'd been looking for.

"You guys should see the sausages!" Cody said, suddenly looming over the table and settling in beside Barbara with a plate he could barely balance in one hand.

"These shrimp crepes are also to die for," Maya said, now next to him. "Get one of those cinnamon rolls too, when you go up there. What were you guys talking about so intensely, like head to head? Or were you just reconnecting over some old times?"

"Old times can be good times," Barbara said, draining her orange juice.

"But not as much if you didn't win," Maya said with a sly smile. "Winning is everything."

"And all the hardboiled eggs were white," Cody added. "Sorry." Another defeat, but the game was far from over. While that threw a blanket over the conversation for a time, it did not shut it down totally. Three minutes later Barbara took it up again while I stood next to her over the fried potatoes at the buffet. Not that she was having any.

She paused over a plate of domestic cheese slices, making no effort to spear one. "Where are you going next?"

My shrug suggested my lack of enthusiasm. "Antigua. That's all we've got for Darren, just an address there and a couple of notes about some problem he had at a bar. He called it a rough night."

"I'd like to come with you." Her manner had subtly changed.

This surprised me. "Don't you have a car?"

"No, I had a driver who brought me up here from Guatemala City in a Mustang. He said we could outrun anyone who tried to mess with us. Single women don't travel these back roads alone, particularly natural blondes. What are you driving?"

I studied her roots. She was the real deal, but I had always known that. "We've got a Nissan Maxima. If your luggage isn't too big, it'll probably work." I picked up a cheese omelet, three huge sausage links, a cinnamon roll and a serving of cottage fries.

"You don't think Maya will object if I come, after all that you and I have been to each other?"

I set down my plate to face her. "And exactly what have we been to each other? You're the most outrageous tease I have ever known and I'm probably the only guy who ever said no to you. I guess you're right, we do have a special relationship." I listened to myself say this, knowing it was the first time I'd ever tried to sum it up. "I'll talk to Maya. How long before you can be ready to go?"

"I'm ready now. I'm always ready, and I think you know that."

Barbara Watt hadn't changed at all. Walking back to the table, it felt like I was edging my way through swampy terrain of a kind I hadn't seen for a while, but it was still awfully familiar. But I already knew that Maya would see Barbara coming with us the same way I did. We needed her for what else she knew, and there would come a time when we would have to pry it out of her. I also knew that when that time came, the one supplying the leverage would be me.

CHAPTER TEN

I was driving when the four of us pulled away around nine-fifteen that morning. Cody was in front for the legroom, and Barbara and Maya shared the back. They could work it out, I thought. After all, we each wanted the same thing: to get to Antigua by the end of the day still on speaking terms and without drawing blood.

After passing a small, secured parking lot near the gate, we pulled onto the highway and headed south. It was already a warm day, cloudless and humid. Not much traffic was in view in either direction. We had gone about three or four kilometers when Cody leaned toward me with his hand partly covering one side of his mouth.

"Remember the white Toyota that was on the ferry crossing the Rio Pasión?"

"Vaguely, kind of a smaller SUV, wasn't it? You thinking of trading in your Ford? A vehicle like that would probably have more leg room."

"No, but that same Toyota was parked in the

guest lot at the gate just now. You know how I have a head for numbers, and I recalled the license plate on that car."

Of course, only Cody would recall a license plate number that he saw just a single time in passing.

"Coincidence?" I said. "People crossing the Rio Pasión are mostly going north, and this would be the main destination before the roads peter out south of the Yucatán border."

"I don't know what it means, maybe nothing. It was just an odd fact, OK? I also recall that he seemed to be in a terrible hurry to get off that ferry."

"I felt the same need once we hit the other side." I drove on another kilometer, simmering about this. "By the way, what was the license number of that big Volvo bus next to us on the ferry?"

He gave it to me without having to stop and think.

The long drive south was not much different from the long drive north, except that late in the afternoon we turned away from Lake Atitlán toward Antigua, which is closer to Guatemala City. Coming back on the Rio Pasión ferry we were accompanied by only one other car and it seemed easier. Two or three hours before we reached Antigua, we had climbed back out of the lowland humidity into a drier and rougher terrain. It was a familiar look; corkscrew roads snaking through the shaved away cliffs that flanked the lumbering dump trucks and impatient chicken buses.

Through this, Maya and Barbara had not had much interaction, possibly because there were witnesses present. We'd had two rest stops, but for a mid day meal we ate the box lunches prepared by the hotel. I wondered whether Barbara was asking herself what we were all thinking. We were certainly wondering that about her. At the end of the afternoon we arrived in Antigua.

I suppose the city must have been constructed on or very near those two combative tectonic plates that divided the country, because the early history of this town as the capital of Guatemala had been cut short by a massive earthquake in the later seventeen hundreds. Others had happened as recently as 1976. Driving in we saw few signs of them, although I'd read there was an old convent that had been partly restored and partly left as it was on the day of the tremor. Not that that was the only one. When we eventually reached the main street, waiting for us at the end was what we could've predicted: a massive volcano. This was Volcán de Agua, which had once filled with water and flooded the town when it erupted again. Imagine a tsunami roaring down the main street at an altitude of 5,000 feet. Nothing I read had suggested it, but I wondered whether the water was boiling.

Yet today's Antigua was a colonial gem of a kind we'd had no hint of so far in Guatemala. Aside from the blocks facing the main square, the buildings were mostly one story. Their condition was admirable, better than in San Miguel in many cases, but my research had told me large parts of the town had languished in ruins for many decades. It must have had a determined restoration effort with a vigorous degree of enforcement behind it, because no gaps were evident. Someone must've made some restoration capital available. I had heard there was an expat community there, and it was easy to see the charm that had persuaded those people to settle in the middle of Guatemala. But if the country offered anything else similar to this small city of 45,000, we hadn't seen it or heard about it.

Maya had booked us into the Porta Hotel Antigua, which had sufficient vacancies to make no problem about adding Barbara Watt to our group.

There were times when Maya liked to score the first point in a new round. Shortly after we settled in she went out among the staff with the photo of Darren and Ixobel. She knew how to project the right balance of class rank and sympathy, and the tone of her Spanish could easily be tuned to the person she was talking with. She also had half a dozen twenty-quetzal notes in her pocket, each worth about $2.75 US. As a tip they were not the end of the world, but we had observed how low wages were throughout Guatemala and they would carry some weight. Giving twice that much for a bit of information would suggest that our search was about more than just looking for an old college buddy rumored to now be settled in Antigua, which is how she planned to present her search.

Cody and I adjourned to a small table in a dim corner of the bar. It had been a long day of driving and we both preferred to start fresh on our quest in the morning. I didn't know where Barbara was. Possibly she craved some alone time, or she might've only been resting. Driving in we had gotten into no discussions of what any of us planned to do on arrival other than collect our luggage and come to earth.

The hotel grounds were spacious and lush with tropical plantings. Like the Garden of the Ancients, there were few walls in the public buildings. This was a touching confidence in the weather that wouldn't have made sense where we lived in San Miguel, a thousand miles north and fifteen hundred feet higher. The pool was large and well attended with a relaxed and casual mood. I was already getting the feeling that Antigua was a unique and atypical part of the fabric of landscape and culture that made Guatemala so different from México.

Cody uttered a prolonged sigh that I could've matched. "The climate here will slow you down if you're not careful."

I brushed this away. "We've never been careful.

That's why we're so good. We were damn good in the Yucatán in spite of the same kind of heat we saw at Tikal. You haven't seen that white Toyota here, have you?"

"No. Not sad about that, either. Maybe that Toyota thing is all in my mind."

"Most things are."

The waiter arrived with our drinks, a planter's punch for Cody and Plantation rum with no ice for me. We both settled back in our wicker chairs. Cody's creaked under his weight. Antigua was starting to grow on me. All you had to do was avoid getting mugged on the way there. For a while I watched the girls at the pool. I had been trained as a lifeguard in college. You never know when the need for those skills will arise, so you must always be ready. I could see a couple that I especially wanted to save, but they didn't seem to be in any distress.

Thirty feet away, on a pair of custom-made perches, two blue and red macaws launched a raucous discussion about dinner. Neither of them was physically restrained, and they could simply have flown away to better pickings if they knew of any. The fact that they chose to remain confirmed my impression of that hotel. "We'll do a thorough check on the address of both Ixobel Bak and Darren Hall in the morning," Cody said.

"And that will produce the same result as calling his cell and emailing him three times a day every day so far since Bernard Emerson's check hit our account."

"Probably. Think of it as procedure. I do. It's not just about handling evidence in a consistent way so you can use it in court; procedure as an investigating method is a process that mostly doesn't give you a result. It mainly tells you what you've eliminated so you can go on to get creative and solve the case through your insight and instinct."

"Two less official but highly effective modes of operating."

"I guess we've proved that many times. What has it given us so far this time?"

Cody shrugged. "It's mostly been the elimination part, but that's what usually comes first."

At that moment Maya spotted us and headed for our table. I tried to read her face as she sat down, but all I got was a mixed outcome.

"How much of that tip money do you have left?" Cody said, more grounded in the process than I was.

"I spent forty quetzales, just two twenty Q notes."

"That's good, five bucks plus a little more. You can buy yourself a drink with what's left, and you deserve it." His arm went up to the waiter. "Now, please share with us what you learned."

"The staff here in the hotel is not eager to talk, but I think I got what we need."

"I like that kind of discretion," I said. "They might be paid better than we think."

"And better pay means more loyalty to your employer."

"Did you mention Darren Hall and his fiancée too?" I said. She had sometimes come up with more than we needed to know in the past, and not enough at other times.

"He was seen here. I spread the photo around to most of the wait staff."

"Did they remember when?"

"The two that recognized him couldn't say exactly. 'A few weeks ago' was the best response I got."

"Was he with anybody?" Cody said. "Or was it only his kinky red hair they remembered?"

"It was that, but also the hair of the woman he was with."

"Seems like Ixobel Bak's hair looks pretty normal for this part of the world," I said. "Possibly it's drawn back a little too tightly, but with those square-rimmed glasses, it gives her an intense kind of focus. The message I got from the photo was that she's attractive and very smart."

May shook her head as if I was missing the point. "They described the woman as *una güera mas bonita*, a most beautiful blonde. A standout, and they remembered Darren Hall mainly because he was having dinner with her. He wasn't a regular diner here."

Cody and I both stared at Maya in silence for a

moment. Our eyes may have held a blank look; an unexpected truth can affect your expression that way. But her face had assumed an aspect of tasteful triumph. I was now anticipating another comment from her about being the head of the Agency and why that was such a good fit when the other two investigators tended to kick back at critical moments such as this.

"Really! And are you suggesting that now *we're* with her too?" Cody said in a startled grumble. "This damn case has got more twists and turns to it than a snake landing on a bed of hot coals." He downed the rest of his drink and flagged the waiter in practically the same gesture. When he came over we asked for menus too, with the second round. Maya treated herself to a cognac. No one protested. Had Bernard Emerson been sitting with us, he wouldn't have objected either, and it was his dime.

Before we ordered dinner I went over to the long two-story row of guestrooms beyond the pool and rang Barbara's bell, thinking she might be ready to explain her prior appearance with Darren Hall over dinner. There was no response, even on the third try. Had she sensed this revelation approaching, knowing she would've been recognized coming in?

I slept well that night, even though normally I'd have been ruminating about Barbara's role in this case.

But we were worn out from traveling all day, and we knew we'd be thinking more clearly in the morning.

Given her relationship to Darren, I was certain we'd be able to persuade Ixobel Bak to talk to us. She must be in a near panic now, but how would we find her? My notes had included only the dead-end contact information that Emerson had given me. In finishing the tale of his investigations, he had made a point of saying again that he had never been able to connect with her. He also had given me Darren's address in Antigua, but he did not believe that he and Ixobel lived together, largely because of family reasons (hers). If this culture was like that of México, most young women still lived at home until they married, not that they didn't find ways to slip away now and then. Being from a prosperous family and having a professional life would introduce more latitude into that equation. There were, of course, well educated independent women, like Maya, who broke all these rules with impunity. I had met her father and stepmother, her wild younger sister, Soledad, and they knew we'd lived together for years. But they were professional and liberal people, and came from a broad strain of anticlericalism in Mexican society. They simply disliked the Church and felt it had long operated with a baneful influence. But we had no information whatever about Ixobel Bak that would give us a clue to her position.

Nor did her doorbell tell us anything more. At

nine-fifteen the following morning Cody and I stood on a numbered street with a nondescript name, something like 3A Calle Poniente, facing a pale single-story green house with a glossy mahogany door. The four pair of closed window shutters were painted a dark slate blue and barred with decorative steel, curling at the bottom and pointed at the top. The effect was coherent and well-planned, and the house appeared prosperous and even mildly upscale. Eventually a maid appeared to answer the door, or at least to enquire what we wanted, because she did not invite us in. Normally conversations between respectable callers and the residents are held inside, in the covered entry, not out on the sidewalk as this one was.

"Señorita Ixobel Bak is not at home," she told us. The woman could not say when she would return.

"Does she still live here?" Cody said.

The maid could not say that either, or would not. Did we wish to leave a message for her?

I handed her my business card and we left. We had not heard another sound from inside the house.

Our next stop was Darren Hall's residence. The address placed it on the east side of town, on Calle de Los Duelos, near a large park. It was a tranquil setting after a pleasant walk. Antigua appeared to be a town where you would rarely need a car, and I hadn't seen any tuc tucs, although I knew there must be some, just as the outskirts of town probably sheltered a tastefully screened depot crammed with chicken buses.

The house was a dry cream-color, almost powdery in tone, with brilliant white trim, a rich but subtle effect. We waited between rings. Cody shifted from one foot to the other.

"I'm getting damned sick of this," he said finally. We'd rung the bell four times. The house remained silent, anonymous.

I knew what was coming, so I turned and leaned against the house so I could watch the street in both directions. A blue pickup approached us from the central district. When it had passed and nothing else came into view, I said, "Let's do it."

Cody pulled out his lock picks and went to work.

"Not bad," he said after a moment. "It's a Bosch, a German deadbolt, and I've seen 'em before. Very exact and precise, you could even call them unforgiving. But once you tickle it in the right place, bingo. You're inside in a heartbeat." And we were. Cody also had a practiced knack for opening and closing a door silently. "If the hinges start to squeak," he'd once told me, "put some lift on it as you open it."

We were standing in a garden that needed watering. Guatemala usually has a decent amount of rainfall, even overwhelming in places, but early signs of neglect showed on many of the plants. The paved courtyard in the center was sprinkled with dead leaves. Along a loggia on the inner side were a wicker sofa with bright cushions, a glass and steel coffee table, and a small round wicker breakfast or dining table with four matching chairs. All was silent.

"Now I'm liking Barbara's kidnapping idea a lot better," Cody said. "Let's check out the lifestyle of a free-lance anthropologist." He threw the hand bolt on the entry door behind us and we moved further inside.

Barbara had not appeared at breakfast either, which was disappointing, since the previous breakfast conversation had been so interesting, if only marginally productive. Maybe she was avoiding us now, because I felt we were getting closer to something relevant. I couldn't have said exactly what.

At the end of the loggia where we went inside was the kitchen. It looked out onto a smaller garden behind, brightly lit at this time of day. If the room was contemporary, it was not precisely modern. I had lost track of those design concepts in my eighteen years in México. We decided to leave it for last. In Latin America kitchens were always a risky place to hide anything, although they often yielded other forms of information. The maid was all over them in ways you could never predict, since she was often hiding things there herself. Besides, why would Darren Hall have anything to hide? I was still trying to think of him as the gentleman researcher, an academic who had come unhobbled from the scholastic herd, a trailblazer off the main intellectual path. I liked that idea, even if I didn't have much confidence in it. Our cases rarely turned out to be about what we wanted them to be about.

The dining room was intimate but richly decorated. It displayed some handsome colonial silver candlesticks on the buffet, but generally it went beyond my taste. I did like the eighteen small antique canvases that lit the walls. Mostly landscapes, they were colonial rather than religious scenes, which most art was in early Latin America. No more than four different painters were represented, so Darren had gone to considerable effort to assemble this group, since they would probably have been dispersed at least 150 years ago. Darren Hall was a man with a considerable level of discernment, I thought.

"So what are we looking at here?" said Cody. The only piece of art in his San Miguel condo was an unsigned LeRoy Neiman football print hanging over the sofa. If you appreciated his slapdash style of brushwork, it functioned in a beefy sort of way. Flanking it were two police length-of-service awards and a citation from his third year on the force for saving a young child from drowning. He'd always worked homicide, but sometimes other opportunities arose.

"I'd say we're looking at a particularly refined place to host a dinner party with a very few close friends and talk about the meaning of..."

"The next NFL draft-pick?"

"Possibly, or possibly not. Although I do think pro football is an anthropologist's dream. A mingling of proven but unassociated tribe members bribed into fielding new blended tribes for even bigger money. The submersion of large individual egos into a group effort. The dynamic of money and power that can inspire that. (What else could?) The access to women who would never have even spoken to them earlier. Not that we've found any sign that Darren was into that aspect of it."

Just off that inviting dining room was an office no larger in scale. It may have been five meters by five again. While on a newish rosewood and steel desk sat a Mac office computer, the real theme of the room, surprisingly, was jade. I had never thought much about jade. Most of it, I knew, came from China. We'd had a case we filed as *The Predator*, where a major jade bowl of Chinese origin played an important role in a Mayan burial, but that had never made me an expert. Maya didn't own any jade jewelry.

When I booted the computer I was not surprised to be shut out by the lack of a password.

On the end of the desk stood a mahogany case about eighteen inches wide that housed a stack of five shallow drawers. Cody slid open the top one. Arranged on a black velvet lining were half a dozen jade ornaments. One was a pale green spiral circlet that coiled in on itself. Two were black amulets with a hieroglyph etched in the center. Every drawer had six or eight pieces in different colors and shapes.

"You would probably know something about this kind of thing," he said. "Do you think they're old?"

I picked up a dark green oval disc from the bottom drawer. About three inches long, it was bored through with a hole near one of the narrower edges. The character of the workmanship was flawlessly smooth and highly polished. It showed no tool marks or abrasions. I shook my head. "I don't know, and I can't think what this stone is worked with. Notice how cold it feels?" I handed it to him. "That says how dense and hard it is. What tools did the ancients have to carve it with? What do we have?" I snapped a shot of each open drawer with my cell and we moved on to the bookshelves that lined two of the walls to a height of about a meter.

Many of the books were focused on art, and not only the arts of Mesoamerica. I saw two books on pre-Raphaelite painting that I also owned in my own library. The Impressionists and post-Impressionists were well represented. Works on Mayan architecture followed, then the Toltec and Olmec styles. Mayan ceramics were amply covered. There were three works on Mayan carved wooden lintels. But I saw nothing by Margaret Meade, and no Joseph Campbell. We found none of the early classic work on the Mayan discoveries, and in fact, no works on anthropology at all, and precious little on archaeology. Was our missing client more a collector than a social scientist?

"Maybe Darren Hall, Ph.D., already knows everything he needs to know about anthropology and he doesn't need any more reference works," Cody said. "He has a mind with qualities that act at once both like a sponge and a steel trap."

"He's a connoisseur," I said, more simply. "Nothing wrong with that." But even to me this sounded thin. Wouldn't he at least have a few favorite classics in his field he could refer to now and then, like if he wanted to quote someone and be sure he'd gotten it right? I pulled out three or four books at random and checked behind them. Sometimes people hid things there, but not this time. I didn't feel like pulling them all out. Putting them back in the wrong order would give away our visit.

We looked around the rest of the room. The desk offered no storage aside from a pencil drawer in the center. It held only pens and pencils and a transparent envelope of Guatemalan postage stamps. The other furniture was either seating or a lamp table. Cody opened the closet door and whistled softly.

Beyond the six panel mahogany door, the entire opening framed a grey Diebold safe. The archaic gilt lettering that identified it suggested it had come from an earlier time, but I suspected that the antique presentation did not mean it would be easy to crack. Naturally a sharp tug at the handle yielded nothing. A wry look covered Cody's face as he reached up and spun the dial a single time, like a greeting to an opponent he knew he was never going to get past.

"Well, just as it was designed to be, this is a stopper for us ordinary burglars. I couldn't get through that door with all the lock picks in the world, and I'm damned good."

"Funny to find that here, though, isn't it? What are we looking at? I know this is a tough country, but what would be the need for this much protection?"

"We're looking at a big steel box made to secure things of real value," Cody said. "At the bottom and the back it's fastened into the house structure. And you know what that tells me? That our finely crafted wooden cabinet of jade trinkets on the desk contains all modern work, because if it was ancient, it would be right here inside this safe."

"Could they be samples?"

He nodded slowly. "Possibly. Samples that show what an artisan could do with different forms and contours, that would demonstrate he was also a master of surface treatment."

"In other words," I said, "someone who although he's a contemporary, is still an artist in his own right."

If there were any files in that office they were on

the computer or in the safe. The rest of the house was a predictable residence for a bachelor with good taste and the money to support it. We found a few feminine items in the bathroom, a pink razor and a popular deodorant, but aside from a woman's white cotton robe in a petite size in the closet, no other women's clothing. Ixobel Bak was discreet. It maybe that she showered here but didn't stay the night.

On the nightstand next to a queen-sized four-poster bed filmy in its drawn back hangings, was a novel by the Victorian writer, Anthony Trollope, one of his Palliser series. This gave me another clue to Darren's taste. He was as retro as his uncle.

Nowhere did we see a laptop, which a lot of people pack to travel with, if they know they're going to be traveling, and if they also know they're about to leave.

Only the kitchen remained, and I confess to being partial to kitchens. They can be a source of clues the owner never thinks he's leaving behind. Since they are supremely a place of domestic business, rather than rage or lust or greed, their owners mistakenly think they reveal nothing about their lives.

The variety of French enameled cookware and the broad range of spices told us at once that the owner was a serious cook. Two bookshelves offered nearly three dozen cookbooks. The cabinets offered no mixes or prepared foods. The pruned down contents of the refrigerator said that Darren was planning to leave for a while, more than only a couple of days. The few food items remaining were those with a long shelf life. There was a jar of Dijon mustard, one half full of capers, and one of Greek olives. No perishables remained. The canister of ground coffee was in the freezer, also a sign of more than an overnight absence. I examined the calendar on the wall near the door. Its monthly cover shots were all of Mayan ruins in Guatemala. Few of the date squares were marked, but paging back into a later part of the February page, I saw this phrase scrawled on a Saturday. *Back in business, I.B.!! Now you're mine.*

That was encouraging, since he'd had some movement, even if we hadn't. But in what sense was Ixobel (if she was I.B.) now his? The bathrobe and toiletries suggested she was not holding him at arm's length. Yet nothing we saw gave us a direction to take for the next step of this case. If I'd needed to file a report for Bernard Emerson as we walked out of the house, it would've been, Darren's not here anymore, and we still don't know where he is, although it sounds like he's gone on to the big time, at least his version of it.

Cody and I were both in a thoughtful mood while he relocked the front door as I watched the street. Walking back toward the hotel, my final insight was that even if our investigating time wasn't, Bernard Emerson's deposit was running out, but as our treasurer, that was

Maya's problem. I wondered what Barbara was up to now. Certainly she was not the only unknown factor in this equation, but certainly the one best represented by the symbol X.

CHAPTER ELEVEN
MAYA SANCHEZ

Alone at her table next to the fireplace, almost shaking in that chilly space with no walls but those that surrounded the kitchen and the bathrooms, Maya started breakfast with a carefully selected plate of local fruits. She had intentionally waited for Paul and Cody to leave before coming down, knowing the path they would probably take. Breaking and entering had never been her most comfortable means of investigation. At best it usually yielded little of merit, and at worst it could be a ticket to jail. She had come from a better family than that in Mexico City. She wanted to consider in solitude the fact that Barbara had dined in this hotel before with Darren Hall. What was she up to then? Probably it was the same thing she was up to now.

The fruit went down well, but it left her with a craving for protein. A couple strips of bacon might warm her up. She pulled the lower corners of Paul's denim jacket around her and went back to the buffet. She had just returned to her table with a cheese and artichoke omelet as well when Barbara Watt sat down beside her with a breathless expression. She set down a similar plate of fruit.

"Hello, darlin'. So those two big detective guys left you here all by yourself. That surprises me so much! You never know who might march right in here and sit down next to you and positively sweep you right off your feet!"

"Go ahead. I'm a detective too." Sensing a fragment of crisp bacon lodged in her back molar on the left as she said this, Maya gave her a level look.

It took Barbara a moment to respond. "But even more, I sense you're kind of like a small, neatly polished rock down here, aren't you, in some ways? And people say Mexicans are so emotional. Like it's hard for them to do business."

"Then try me. At home we throw stones to drive off the street dogs. That's what rocks can do, even the polished ones. Somehow the sharp edges remain, and they can take the street dogs down. Believe me."

A long uncomfortable moment of silence followed.

Barbara set down her fork with emphasis. "I absolutely know that I've told you before that I never screwed Paul, not a single time, no matter how much he wanted it."

Maya smiled dimly, picturing this no matter how much she hated the idea. "And I've always liked your nobility and your honor, in that way, more than any other part of you. Knowing when someone's longtime boyfriend is off limits."

"Thank you for recognizing that! Now I feel like we're finally communicating at last."

"I love that too! So let's push it a little further. Tell me then why you're down here. I understand it's not your first trip."

Barbara returned a delicate shrug. "Well, quite naturally, anyone touring Guatemala would love to see Antigua. It's such a colonial jewel."

"Of course. So what brought you back this time? Were you hoping to meet Darren Hall for dinner here again? It must've surprised you that I booked us here."

At that moment a server came by to refill their coffee. Maya could see Barbara was thinking hard. When the server moved on, Barbara placed her elbows on the table and leaned forward, clasping her hands. "I believe I'm going to have to be frank with y'all."

"I do know that I'm ready for that."

"I've known Darren Hall for several years. I have used him to vet, shall we say, some of the artifacts I've been offered from Central America, not many, of course. I don't know if you realize he's something of an expert."

"I didn't. That sounds a little beyond the bounds of

ordinary anthropology."

"Who can say? When you know the culture to the degree he does, it's not just about dating rituals and marrying inside or outside your own clan. You develop an intimate feel for their *stuff*, too, do you know what I mean? The texture of it, the coldness of it in your hand, for example."

"And the Mayans had really good *stuff*, didn't they, Barbara?"

She nodded solemnly. "The best. Trust me on that."

"We're not talking about textiles here, are we?"

"No, this country is the only source of real jade in the Americas. The Mayans knew it, and they knew how to work it. Not all of it has been recovered from the tombs by any means."

"You came down here to make sure you get your share, isn't that true?"

"Yes! If you insist on putting it that way. And who is a better conservator than I am? I've proven it before and I think you already know that."

"You do have the means." Barbara had inherited $40 million when her husband Perry died during the Zacher Agency's first case. Two similar bequests had gone to his children from an earlier marriage. "And you have the climate controlled facility in your house for any artifacts that might come your way."

"Exactly, it goes from deep frost to..."

"Too hot to handle," Maya said, smoothly. "Has Darren Hall come across something for you, or is he vetting an object you recently bought?"

"I only wish it was that simple. He emailed me very early in March that he had obtained one of the great jade burial masks of Tikal." She speared a small chunk of cantaloupe and placed it in her mouth.

Although she quickly tossed down her coffee, Maya couldn't block the chill that flowed through her body. "That must have gotten your attention. Obtained is an interesting word in that context."

"True, but words like that never get any more specific in this business. You can get old here waiting for a real provenance to emerge. If you're satisfied it's the real deal, then you grab it. If the artifact is genuine, that's always the best it's ever going to get. Who really owns it is an abstraction, merely a matter of a written title. Go out into the market and see who's offering a title on the tuc tucs for sale, or the chicken buses. This is all about what works. Things go from hand to hand and no one has the time or money for a registered title. The governing word today in this country is possession, just as it has always been."

This neither troubled nor offended Maya. In México, the entire country had been seized by the Conquistadores in the sixteenth century by an unprecedented act of de facto possession. The titles all came later, signed first by the Church, and countersigned by the government after a suitable pause.

"So how did you respond to Darren when he said that?"

"Naturally, I said, stop the presses and don't tell another soul. I'm coming to get it now. I am literally packing and on my way out the door, and you know I'm good for it."

"And what did he say?"

Barbara appeared to wilt slightly. "He said he had received another offer for it, but he felt because of all the business we'd done, he had to offer it to me first."

Maya recalled that Barbara had earlier said she'd never bought any contraband antiquities in Guatemala, but had modified that once or twice later. "But he hadn't exactly done that, had he? Did he say what the offer was or who it came from?"

"No, and I haven't heard anything more from him."

"So how do you know what else developed? Who could've told you? Why did you need to come back here?"

"I was still in San Miguel getting ready to come down here when I received a cryptic email from Ixobel Bak. I had met her here twice before through Darren."

Maya leaned forward over the table. "What did

she say?"

Barbara glanced from side to side, but no one was close enough to hear. "She said, 'Darren has disappeared and I'm going to look for him. I know you're planning to come down, so join me if you wish, but you'll need to bring plenty of money.'"

Maya made a noncommittal gesture. "But you always bring plenty of money."

"Yes, but I sensed that she meant *real money*."

"Was there any more?"

"I asked her when she had last seen him. She said that two days before he had stopped by her house at about nine in the evening. He was on his way to the Blue Gazelle and asked her if she wanted to come along. She said no. It wasn't a place she cared to go to, since it was always full of tourists. Since he was long past that kind of thing, she recalled wondering why he wanted to go, but she hadn't asked him."

CHAPTER TWELVE

Bring down some real money and head out to a tourist bar in the town where Darren's lived for years," said Cody. Maya had given us her report and we'd given her ours on our home visits. I was surprised she'd gotten that much out of Barbara, but our passenger must've thought it was time to contribute something useful just to stay aboard.

"That potentially opens a door with a lot of bad things happening behind it," Cody said.

"Maybe this Blue Gazelle place could be the key," I said. "We're working tourists, more or less, so we don't have to make a lot of effort to fake it. All we have to do is appear to know less than we do."

"That might take some effort; that's already a very small area."

Maya had left us after lunch, pleading a tour of some of the upscale shops in town. Bar crawling was much like lock picking to her; it was not her idea of investigating.

"I'm recalling something now," I said, "and I can dig it out again if I have to, but Emerson's original letter referred to 'a rough night in Antigua.' I could find it easily enough, I know it's up in my suitcase, but I'm sure that's the exact quote."

"He didn't say where, though, in Antigua?"

"No. It could've been Ixobel's father calling Darren out to account for his extended relationship with his daughter without setting any date for the wedding."

"So what have we got now?"

"Sure, I can get that," I said. With my college minor in history, I was often in charge of the case progress recaps when Maya wasn't present. "Emerson can't find Darren. We established that he's not in his house here in Antigua. Ixobel, who won't talk to us either, is going to look for him and invited Barbara to help with adequate funds. In the meantime no one is home, people don't answer their email messages, and when I send Bernard an email report, he has little to say in response, as if he's not sure it's worth it so far. And, as Maya would say, we're running out of money, our initial retainer."

"Money is the great lubricant of both crime and law enforcement," said Cody. "They are the evil twins. But why would Darren go to a tourist bar? At home in San Miguel we all steer clear of them. If you visited one there you would never see anyone you recognized."

I started nodding because suddenly I knew. "It's

the very thing you just said. Anonymity. You pick a place to meet someone where nobody knows your name. Anyone who saw you there could only give a physical description, and as you've seen many times in court, witnesses can often be a couple of degrees off in what they recall, or even more."

"But didn't he ask Ixobel to come along that night?" Cody said. "Why would he want her there if he was up to something he wanted to hide from her?"

"Yes, so he must've asked her knowing she wouldn't come. It was like he was scattering crumbs in his path. If something went wrong, she could testify later where he had gone and why she hadn't come with him, and what time it was, just as Barbara told us."

"The Darren Hall you're describing sounds fairly devious."

"We're not easily disillusioned," I said.

"No, but it does happen."

It was later afternoon, approaching cocktail hour, and we were strolling along 3 Avenida Sur (South Third Avenue), where we hoped to find the Blue Gazelle. When it appeared, it was easy to pick out from all the nicely restored one-story colonial buildings. For one thing, it looked like a ruin. It probably really had been part of a ruin, but I guess that's not a bad thing here. All the recovered buildings played nicely against the exposed shells of those that were unrestored.

The outer walls of the Blue Gazelle were a jumble of thin red brick, rubble, and dressed stone, originally assembled with the knowledge that they would never be seen again once they were faced with stucco. It's the kind of structural illustration you get when the surface plaster falls away over time, or more likely here, when it's violently shaken off. It was a perfect fit in a town where any snapshot of ancient exposed walls reveals the same random texture. To me, it was a reminder of the perpetual vulnerability of this geographic location. Living here, I thought, we'd want to always be in a tent, where the weight of collapse didn't amount to much. We are, after all, tiny creatures set precariously against the gargantuan forces beneath us.

Inside, the bar was all about exposed brick, cattle skulls, and handcrafted furniture made from exotic jungle hardwoods. Thick smoky candles lurked in colored glass holders. It was a transplanted 1970s fern bar with hippy overtones, missing only a few stained glass lamps. Behind the main room was a small courtyard lacking a couple of big umbrellas to repel the late afternoon sun. It was a shame that neither Cody nor I played Foosball. Still, the big flat screen television over the bandstand caught his eye, even turned off.

We sat down at a small but quite tall cocktail table. It was a place for an intimate conversation if you could keep your balance on the tiny stools. Possibly after a couple drinks you'd want to move closer to the floor while such a move was still under your control. A waitress came past and slapped down a pair of drink menus. She was a redhead with ample freckles and a pastel green headscarf knotted at the back of her head. A few curled strands escaped over her forehead. For me, the colors were a good mix. She knew it. The tiny gold ring piercing her left nostril might even have been gold. Her minimal tank top suggested that her freckles traveled everywhere over her very pale skin. This was clearly a woman who needed to work at staying out of the sun.

I leaned over in her direction. "Berkeley," I said, "political science. You're lacking only a few credits to finish, but you plan on going back very soon."

She waved me off. "Not even close! Archaeology. Not a bad pickup line, though."

It was my turn to shrug. But why not play a bit? What else was there to do here?

"Lisa," she said, holding out her hand. I could see that she chewed her fingernails. That wasn't a turn on, but there are worse vices. We'd come across most of them.

"He and I are just tourists," I said, pointing at Cody. "We needed to come to earth somewhere and this place caught our eye."

"Sure, not a problem. We get a lot of gay people in here. Antigua's a tolerant kind of place, you know, even if the rest of the country isn't. You won't have any trouble if you don't get too noisy later on."

"Thank you for that," Cody said, leaning over the table toward her without missing a beat. "We've got some straight friends here and we haven't been able to find them. We met them in a bar in Guatemala City, but they told us that the Blue Gazelle was where it was all going down in Antigua. We just had to check it out."

"Did they give you one of our coupons?" she said.

"Ah, no. Did we miss out on something?"

"Sure, because Preston at the bar gives people coupons to hand out to other people they meet. When somebody uses one of them, he reads their name off it and they have a free drink credit at the bar when they come back."

"We missed that. I can tell you his name though," I said. "Maybe you saw it on one of those coupons. It was Darren Hall." I pulled out his photo and handed it to her.

Feathering her lips with two fingers, Lisa studied it for a moment. "Not someone I know, although I may have seen her. What does he do?"

"He's an anthropologist." I felt suddenly queasy saying this. Was I contributing to his myth in some way?

"Let me ask around." She went off to fill our order and left the photo on the table.

Cody and I remained alone on our stools. "Is that the first time we've been picked out as a couple?" he said.

"To our face, at least. You never know the rest."

After about forty-five minutes we moved to a lower table and ordered some snacks from a different server. Lisa had never returned with a report, so I assumed she hadn't discovered anyone that knew Darren, if she'd even tried. The crowd was building, mostly people in their twenties and thirties. We heard snippets of sports talk around us, not soccer, but U.S. basketball and football teams. They didn't seem like vacationers, although some must've been. If they were residents, how did they earn an income? I estimated the cost of living to be twice what it was in San Miguel, but even so a bit cheaper than in the States.

"I can't get that statement of Emerson's out of my mind," I said, "'a rough night in Antigua.' How rough does this place get? Outside of its crumbly exterior the Blue Gazelle could be located on the edge of some middling college campus in Ohio. Tonight it looks like the week before finals and none of the students can bring themselves to study yet."

"Sure, it's too early for them to panic," Cody said. "As I think back, I was often driven by panic at exam time. That was an excellent preparation for my job in homicide, as I found out later. It taught me that calmness was the state of mind that worked best in a crisis. To this day, it still is."

"I'm calm," I said, wishing I had more reason not to be.

From the main room behind us the sound of instruments tuning up reached our ears. After a moment they broke into *Hotel California*, which cast a slightly surreal mood over the scene. An American woman, or perhaps Mexican American, walked toward us, wearing a short jungle print sundress and sandals. Her bracelet, earrings, and necklace were all jade beads. I noticed this before anything else. Her hair was dark and thick, cut short in not quite a bob. The other thing that caught my eye was her wide expressive mouth, bracketed at the corners with tiny animated lines like parentheses. She might have been thirty-five, and she paused at our table for no reason I could think of, but we were both willing to listen as she pulled up a chair unasked.

"Gay men rarely look at me like you just did, OK? Lisa said I should talk to you. Should I try to change your mind?" But she wasn't speaking to me.

"You already have," Cody said. "I feel like I'm crossing over that line right now. His index finger traced a big X on the tablecloth."

"It's called going bi."

"I'm ready. Just tell me what to do next."

"Sure. Start by burning all your Liza Minnelli CDs."

His right hand made a horizontal gesture as if sweeping something from the table. "Done. Did it before I left home, although in my head I was still listening to that one about *New York, New York* on the way down here."

Because I liked her manner, I gave this woman a broad smile. After all, she had scored all the points so far, and success is one of my values. Cody obviously didn't mind her, either. "I want to know who I'm talking to. My name is Paul Zacher and this is my friend Cody Williams. We're here on vacation."

"I heard it was a vacation with a mission."

"Everything comes with missions in Latin America," I said. After all, we'd had extensive experience with it. "I'd like to know your name."

"Normally I don't say it until much later in the evening."

"I'm sure," I said, "and that's your choice. But even if it's still early to take our masks off, this is the tipping point. You have something to tell us and we have an interest in your story. You know how there is a moment when you can go public with a story that has real meaning? If you decline to do that the truth is never told."

"Or it's told by someone else who will never get it right in the way that only you could," Cody said.

She gave us a brilliant smile that was all teeth, and good ones. "And does the truth matter all that much?

Not that it doesn't matter in the moment to you, but I mean in a larger sense, to the rest of us who aren't being paid to make reality work for a client?"

Well, it does when you're being paid by the hour, but I didn't care to say that. Truth usually comes in small chunks to us. Our task is to assemble them into a case we can use. The adhesive we need to do that varies widely, and I found that I didn't care to suggest to her what that was. I already knew she had her own. "Let me buy you a drink and you can talk to us," I said. How did she know we were being paid for this?

"My name is Carolina, and I'll take a good bourbon, up. Can I see that photo you showed Lisa?" Cody pulled it out and set it in front of her while I flagged the waiter. She nodded immediately. "What a funny shot this is, with them off looking at something else, but that's Ixobel Bak and her *novio*, Darren. She's a friend of mine. I know him too, but not so much."

While this was useful information, and worth some further exploration, I found myself staring again at her jade jewelry, beads in a variety of colors ranging from black to white with a wide array of greens between. They were also graded in size. The finish was clearly a match with the pieces in Darren's sample case, if that's what it was. I wasn't sure how to read this. Was there only one way to polish jade, and therefore the surfaces of all of it looked nearly the same? Or was this a distinctive look, so these beads had come from the same hand as the samples?

"There must be a wonderful source of jade here," I said, "and I'm admiring your beads. I think I read once that jade mining and working has only recently come back to life in Guatemala, like within the last generation or two." This was only a guess.

Carolina's hand went to her necklace and she nodded. "There is a man here who does the most exquisite work, just like the ancients. Of course, he's Mayan himself. He was trained in an established workshop, but he broke away and went on his own. These beads were all made of the scraps from larger pieces. Nothing is ever wasted."

"He must be a very talented individual," said Cody. The waiter returned with her bourbon.

As she took a careful sip, she gave him a thoughtful look. "Yes, but he's also got a lot of rough edges. That's why he couldn't survive in the studio where he was trained. Perhaps you know some people who are genuine artists; they're not always easy to live with, or even be around."

"I've heard that too," I said. "They can be difficult at times." We'd known one or two who fit that description in a case we'd filed not so long ago as *The Jericho Journals*. I had a sudden idea. "I wonder if that jade artist ever comes down here to unwind at the end of a long day? Even if it's an American style sports bar with some retro music. That might be a good break for him."

"Well, Chucho is a sports nut, and in fact, he does come down here now and then. That's how I met him. He lived in the States for a while and he got into football there."

"I suppose he could've run into Darren here too," Cody said.

She gave him a veiled look. "You sound like you know something."

"Just a little. I can always handle more. Anyway, football's my game too. Always has been."

"Who do you like?"

"Anyone who's winning. College or pro? Tell me a year."

I gave him a quick glance to try to steer him off that. "At our hotel, we talked to another friend of Darren's who told us he'd run into some trouble here one night." In mid sentence I had found myself reluctant to use Bernard Emerson's name. I wasn't sure why. Carolina leaned in toward us.

"I know what you're talking about. Chucho and Darren had a real dust up here one night. I wasn't there but Ixobel told me about it later. She didn't know the exact cause, but it was something about money. Apparently Chucho had made some things for Darren and he wanted to be paid more than the up front estimate he'd given him."

"Had Darren used Chucho before to make things for him?" Cody said.

"I don't know. I didn't know either of them that well. You could ask Ixobel."

"Do you remember when that dust-up was?" I said, thinking it interesting that Carolina spoke of Darren in the past tense.

"Yes, it was more or less some time late in March. It could've been early Aril. Darren left right after that."

"Didn't he disappear?" said Cody. "By that I mean did he slip away without telling anyone where he was going or even that he was going? Not even telling Ixobel, in this case."

"Has Ixobel heard from him at all?" I said.

Carolina shook her head slowly, looking back and forth at both of us. "I don't think so, and now she's gone too. You probably already knew that, I think, didn't you? And who did you say you were again?"

CHAPTER THIRTEEN

It was only about 8:30 when we returned to the hotel. We separated and Cody settled in at the bar for a nightcap and I found Maya in our room. She was not unhappy to have eaten dinner by herself. Group travel could make her wish for some alone time, especially when the group included Barbara Watt. I could see that. She'd sent off an update to Bernard Emerson with more detail than I'd been giving him, and asked for another deposit for time on the clock and expenses. She asked for the same amount, $5,000 U.S. We'd been burned enough before so that now we always tried to keep the cash flow current with the billings. He hadn't quibbled and said he would wire it into our account first thing in the morning.

"Did he seem happy?" I said. "Or at least, satisfied in a provisional way?"

"In that kind of grudging style that he has, where reality is always coming up a little short of his hopes, I guess he was OK. Maybe that's as good as he ever gets."

"He needs a good woman to share his triumphs."

"Was tonight a triumph? Did you and Cody meet some babes?" Maya's command of English slang was always important to her.

"Carolina was not bad, but tonight she was more of an information source than a flirt. As a friend of Ixobel Bak's, she gave us a little background on the 'rough night in Antigua' theme." I filled in the detail for Maya.

"So Ixobel is gone now too. I know you couldn't find her at home."

"Barbara had said the same thing. This is only confirmation. Nice to have that much, though. Ixobel has gone after Darren."

We moved out onto the covered terrace of our room. From there the lighted pool in the center of the grounds was partially visible through the thick vegetation. The birds were settling down in the branches with their usual bickering. Maya disappeared for a moment and then returned with two glasses of wine. We settled back into wicker chairs with impressive cushions. She was close enough so I could take her hand.

"You know, when Cody and I showed her that photo, Carolina pointed out something to us that I had noticed before, but I hadn't given it any special importance. Now I wonder why I didn't."

"Sure. Darren and Ixobel are not looking at the camera. I noticed that too."

I stared at her for a moment. "Did that bother

you at all?"

"At first, but then I tried to imagine why that would be. Suppose it was a big fiesta, and everyone was interacting with a number of people. Some were passing the table and greeting them. Darren was trying to light a cigar. Bernard might have taken half a dozen photos, not all of them posed, like you said, and to give us he chose the one that had the clearest resemblance. It wasn't an art shot or a memorable portrait."

"This photo is quite clear." I again pulled it out of my pocket.

"There you go. I felt that too."

We didn't talk for a while. I didn't mind winding down either. When the character of your business is that little is happening, it can be equally as trying as chaos.

"How was Barbara at dinner?"

"At her least offensive. She wasn't there." With a brief swirl of her glass, Maya finished it.

"That raises a question. Where was she?"

"Barbara doesn't tell me anything, and why should she? Maybe she doesn't like my company any more than I like hers. You always want to think you're the glue that holds this agency together, but maybe it's only spit and good will; nothing that would hold up in a high wind. I can sense a storm coming, a *tormenta*."

"You probably noticed that Emerson's hat had a chin strap on it. He was ready when he hired us."

I wondered if the part about spit and good will was a Mexican expression I had somehow missed in my eighteen years of residence. It was possible. Perhaps it came from somewhere nearer to the Gulf than where we lived. We had seen our share of high winds, and our present location didn't offer much protection for future blasts. Whether any more were coming in this case, I couldn't have said. It was mostly a situation where no one we wanted to talk to was available. In that respect, it looked like a lot of other cases. Just as we felt we were spinning in neutral they had a way of breaking out abruptly when we least expected it.

"What is she doing, Barbara, I mean?"

Maya shrugged. "She's letting us be her chauffeur." She gave this the Mexican pronunciation, *chofer*.

"But she tosses us an occasional crumb or two."

"That's all. Has she offered to pay for any gas? No. Has she offered to drive? No. Has she given us more than two peso's worth of information?"

"At least she's not hitting on me all the time like before."

"Isn't she?" Maya handed me her empty glass. "You don't see her when your back is turned. But maybe you don't have to. I know you have a perfect visual memory. Without turning you will see her eyes following you from a kilometer away."

"Let's not go there." I rose and went inside to

pour us more wine.

When I returned a moment later Cody was seated in my chair.

"Where did you see it?" Maya was saying.

"It was parked on that street that runs along the west side of the main plaza. I didn't feel like staking it out. It may be nothing but coincidence."

"The white Toyota SUV," I said without enthusiasm and repeated the license number perfectly.

"Now you know it too?"

"How could I not?" I said. "I want to be sure it's the right one if I spot a car like that."

"I'll have what you're having."

I went back inside to pour out the last of the bottle for him.

"At least the next move is simple," I said when I returned. "All we have to do now is find out where Ixobel went. Then she will take us to Darren. She knows the country, she knows her boyfriend, and she knows the backstory of this case, none of which is true of us."

"I wonder if that email message from Ixobel to Barbara, the one that brought her down here, told Barbara where to go if she wished to follow her trail with those packs of real money?" Cody said. "You will recall that she didn't tell us her destination, only that it was that message that brought her down here."

"I'll go down to the lower level now and see if

she's at home," I said. "She'll probably answer the door to me before either of you." Not sure I should've said that, I finished my glass and went down the stairs at the center of the building. Her room was three spaces along in our direction, but after I knocked three times she still wasn't answering. No light leaked from under the door, and like México, they don't use thresholds in Guatemala. I put on my spur-of-the-moment wanderer face and drifted through the grounds, the casual American tourist just a bit off his game in this semi-exotic country. If I'd had the luxury of a wardrobe change for this scene, I would've been wearing shorts, which most adult men don't do in Latin America. The pool was now empty but for two fifteen-year-old boys slapping water at each other, and while the bar was full, none of the tables offered me Barbara or anyone like her. The restaurant was still busy, but my casual walk through yielded no one I knew. It was time for plan B.

At the front desk I walked up to the desk clerk with a nervous look, glancing at my watch. "I was planning to meet Barbara Watt here tonight at 8:30 and now I can't locate her. I'm sure she said she was staying in this hotel, because it's one of her favorites. Can you check which room she's in?"

"But of course, *señor*. One moment, please." He scanned his computer screen for a second. "Oh yes, she was in 12B, but unfortunately she checked out earlier today. I am so sorry! Can I help you with anything else?"

Feeling a different phase of the Darren Hall case coming on, I thanked him with less enthusiasm.

CHAPTER FOURTEEN

Information always costs money, and sometimes it costs a great deal of money, depending on your resources and your choices. For example, after shutting down my favorite watering hole, should I run that red light at two in the morning or not? Or, when should I draw my gun as two gangbangers creep up on me? Will they both draw theirs at the same time? Our clients know this and anyone who trades the stock market knows it perhaps more painfully than the rest of us. When for example, is it time to get out of that sure-thing high-flier uranium mining stock your dentist told you about that hasn't yet left the nest although it's lost half the price you paid for it? That is the real cost of information. You never want to sell the bottom, but what is the bottom? Ask Bernard Emerson, who was already in this game for $10,000, and he knew little more than he did when we came into it. Was the Paul Zacher Agency the bottom? I had a few reasons for not believing that.

At other times you know that information is

going to cost you, but you can't even find the booth to pay your tab. That costs you too, extra. Operating far from your home base predictably amplifies this risk.

This uncomfortable but all too familiar situation was where the Agency now found itself. Over many cases I had come to regard it as *The Dead Zone*, named for a horror movie I had once seen on Netflix. Fortunately we had been on more of a (semi-confident) roll when Maya extracted the second $5,000 batch of greenbacks from Bernard Emerson. By the following morning they had hit our checking account with more momentum than any of us possessed anymore in the case.

We were holed up in a very pleasant but somewhat pricy hotel in a lovely colonial town with nowhere to go and no clue as to our next move. Truthfully, that situation had often before felt like home in the middle of many of our cases. We even took some solace in the fact that our lack of performance had a reassuringly familiar appearance, if only to us.

"This is how we always look on the verge of triumph," we would say heartily at breakfast, toasting each other with orange juice that left a slightly sour aftertaste, and stopping somewhat short of slapping each other on the back. At least Barbara Watt was no longer there to witness this. It was the next morning at breakfast and we were again reviewing the report I'd delivered the evening before.

"It was nice of Barbara to tell us she was leaving," Maya said, as if reading my thoughts.

"What I'm most importantly seeing in her exit, and call me a Pollyanna," Cody said, "is that she didn't leave with us, whatever you think of her manners or her sense of gratitude. I believe that means she left with someone else. For me there is information in every situation, no matter how bleak it looks."

"You're saying that she must have asked around to find that other person," Maya added, "unless she already had someone's name when we arrived. But she didn't know we were coming here, and she surely didn't know she'd be riding with us from the Garden of the Ancients in Flores."

This sent us off on a new tangent. After breakfast Maya took on the person at the reception desk, I took the concierge, and Cody covered the staff people at the entry. Only Cody came up with anything.

"It cost me a hundred quetzales," he said. "Not quite fourteen bucks. At least it was not hard to describe who I was talking about."

"And where did she go?" I said.

"She's going to Livingston."

Maya and I both shrugged. "Sounds like a place in Belize," she said, "which used to be called British Honduras before independence. I think it still has a lot of towns with English sounding names."

"No, they told me it's in Guatemala, and on the Caribbean coast. It's something called a Garifuna town."

"So it's an African and Caribe mix," Maya said, writing down Cody's latest bribe in the expense notebook.

"And that's more than halfway across the country," I said, trying not to groan. "Again."

"It gets worse. They told me there's no longer any road you can use to drive to Livingston. It's only approachable by water. Normally you would come from along the south side of the Río Dulce as far as Puerto Barrios, where there's a river taxi that brings you across to the northern side of the estuary and Livingston in about twenty minutes. But now there's a hitch. The road to Puerto Barrios was cut by a landslide four days ago, and you can't reach it by land anymore except from Honduras."

I shook my head. "Bernard Emerson is not paying us enough to go into Honduras, and I can't imagine Barbara is planning to do that either. After all, didn't she need some hotshot bodyguard with a Mustang to get her up to Flores unmolested?"

"Anyway, the guys in front of the hotel hooked her up with a local driver who was willing to do the trip. He'll take her to San Felipe de Lara, an old fortress town located at the point where the Río Dulce comes out of Lake Izabal, and there she can take the day ferry as it heads back down to Livingston. It makes a complete circuit, starting in Livingston in the morning, getting into San Felipe around noon, and ending back in Livingston for the night."

"That sounds simple enough," said Maya. "Has she lost her mind?"

"It made sense to me when they explained it," Cody said. "I didn't think she'd be traveling on the one of those chicken buses. Not with her nice luggage."

"She should've hired another bodyguard," Maya said.

"So that has to be where Ixobel was headed," I said. "I wonder what the charm of Livingston is? It's got isolation and good proximity to the Belize border if she needs to go somewhere else in a hurry. She must have heard or at least suspected that Darren had gone there. It's going to be steamy on the Caribbean this time of year."

There was no reason to delay our start, and the drive looked like it could take two days, subject to the highway conditions. We packed up our things, checked out, and hit the road for San Felipe de Lara, hoping to catch the river ferry for Livingston by noon the following day. Maya was driving. Knowing what we knew by then, we would've been better off asking Bernard Emerson to pay us by the kilometer instead of the hour. That way the huge distance totals we'd racked up would be far more impressive than our results in trying to find Darren Hall.

A little over an hour and a half later, once we'd passed the pulsating bulge of Guatemala City, which slowed us down a bit, we headed further east and slightly north. The country was not much different from what we'd gone through on the way up to Tikal, tapering roughly through ragged canyons toward gradually dropping altitudes, leveling out into a slowly growing proportion of workable farmland mixed with uncleared patches of jungle.

Once again, the villages were often terribly poor. The chicken buses were predictably wacky and often managed to be downright stylish in a free-spirited way, with a kind of carnival desperation. Despite the poverty and lingering residue of civil war and repression, elements of infectious joy broke out now and then. Many people were getting by and even enjoying themselves. I saw a lot of laughter in the small town markets as we passed. Even as it displayed their contrary enjoyment of life it also revealed the gaps in their teeth.

Part of it, I had read, was that the current president, Jimmy Morales, was quite popular. Starting out with degrees in business and theology, he had spent years as a television comedian, and campaigned on a platform of no more corruption. I'm surprised he survived running on a radical stance of that kind. Some members of the previous administration were even now in prison.

After a long run on widely variable roads, where our conversation was little more than speculation, we spent that night in a town whose name I wrote down in our expense journal, but as I make these notes some weeks later back in San Miguel, I cannot now recall, since Maya keeps all the detailed expense records in her archive. But it was a waypoint like many others, a neutral stopover lacking any distinction in a country full of character, not all of it inviting or even benign. It probably set a new standard for unmemorable places.

Reading this back, it occurs to me that I've come down rather hard on Guatemala. I don't say *too hard*. Other than the seductive charm of Antigua, with its freshly painted facades mixed with the stark antique ruins and the great, if often threatening beauty of the local volcanoes, it did not capture my affection. It's too tough on visitors, too hard on its residents, and unless Jimmy Morales can start a dynasty of benign rulers, the ordinary people will continue to be misruled after his departure. They deserve far more than they've been given until recently. The Mayans have long been a noble race, and they warrant better treatment than what the heirs of the Conquistadores have usually offered them over the past 500 years.

In an "Are we there yet?" frame of mind, at about one o'clock the following afternoon The Paul Zacher Agency reached San Felipe de Lara. There, paused at the waterline with its long concrete pier, we were twenty minutes too late to catch the river ferry, which had already hit its turn around point, offloaded and reloaded, and was now steaming back down the Rio Dulce to the coastal towns of Puerto Barrios and Livingston without us. None of us in the Agency were in a mood to wait another twenty-four hours for its return. The thought of Barbara Watt already in place on the other end working her obscure magic without us was hard to take. She still knew more than we did, even though no one was paying her to investigate this case. That made me wonder what the jackpot might be for her. She had never in her life been a penny ante player.

In contrast, the shack of the harbormaster resembled something from a back lot set of The *African Queen*, but with a more advanced case of jungle rot. Beneath the rusted corrugated sheet metal roof, the weather-scoured plank exterior was, I could tell from my woodworking days, constructed of some lovely exotic wood, now grayed and cracked from its unforgiving outdoor service. In need of darning, a faded windsock drooped weakly above the structure like a pathetic trophy from a livelier place, as if shoreline breezes or changing tides could ever make a difference this far up the estuary of the Río Dulce.

At the point between the river's beginning and the huge lake behind it, the centuries old restored fortress offered serene battlements and polished cannons. This remote place had mattered once.

The harbormaster emerged and approached us with an assertive step. "You have meesed the only ferry for today, *señores*," he said, in fairly clear English, clearer than my Spanish probably sounded to him at that moment. We had not been hearing Mexican Spanish here, although the local version wasn't so far off.

I took a strong step toward him. Without being precisely aggressive, my height of a fraction of an inch over six feet works well in a country where the men are mostly five-foot six. "I must tell you that we need to get to Livingston quickly." I said this in a tone of barely controlled urgency. "We have a close family member there who is very ill. I'm sure you have had a medical emergency here before, so you can suggest a solution more advantageous than the ferry we just missed. One that doesn't stop at every little fishing dock along the way would be the best solution for us."

He chuckled as if *quickly* were an archaic term he had once looked up in the English/Spanish dictionary a long time ago, and was now amused to hear that it was still in actual use today, mostly among uninformed people. After only this long in Guatemala, I wasn't sure why it was still current myself. I hadn't come across it much in México, so why would I think anyone here might find a use for it? Maybe it was simply a kind of polite slang whose literal meaning was long gone, and had taken on an entirely different connotation. Although it was still called the same thing, it now might mean something rather different, like a marker to identify people who didn't belong here.

"In that case I have much good news for you. My cousin Luis has a large boat with many seats."

"How many?" I said, not surprised by his cousin's name. Clearly, any branch office we might establish down here would have to be called the Luis Zacher Agency, if only to fit in.

"I think with eight seats. It could be. I don't take it for myself, so I don't always count."

"Of course, but it has a canopy?" Maya said, thinking of her skin tones.

"One that goes, *señora*, as I know, all the way from the front to the back."

That certainly made sense in this climate. As in México, no local residents here wanted to darken their skin unnecessarily. "I have to believe that your primo (cousin) Luis has many years of experience on the river doing this same service," I said, making a gesture as if good fortune were now raining upon my head. Privately I wondered if this man we were speaking to had ever really met Luis.

"More than you are old," he replied. More than the gray hairs on your chin, was his literal response in

Spanish, but I don't like the way that sounds. The only time I ever grew a beard, in my twenties, it looked like pubic hair, as few women failed to point out at the time. Even some I didn't know.

"I am sure his family is extensive and healthy," I replied, trying to assess the approaching level of risk.

"Yes, and they all depend on him for their living, since three of his children are still in school. He is a careful family man, full of the respect from his community too, as well as the strangers that he is honored to serve from this pier." He gestured toward the bleak concrete installation lined with white-painted tires on ropes that protected the boats moored on both sides.

But who else would be able to say that? Bunch of itinerant buccaneers that we were, certainly none of us in the Agency could've given that response with a straight face.

The harbormaster led us inside. He had a computer in his office with one of those ancient black forty-pound monitors tapering front to back that I had started to notice accumulating in Mexican landfills about ten years before. He punched in a few keys. Like square plastic mushrooms on stalks, each one made its own distinct click. I was reminded that Internet responses were still called clicks today because of equipment like this.

"You are so generous to do this," Maya said, eyeing the paraphernalia with veiled chagrin. Surely the twentieth century had arrived here with huge impact, but had not yet been replaced. Usually when she'd overused this line in the past, she'd been sporting a much shorter skirt, but, as she had often reminded me, you cannot be prepared to dress for every occasion when you're on the road. Like this one, challenging situations can come upon you with no warning, and travel anywhere is inherently an inefficient occupation. This reminded me of Cody's process in Guatemala City trying to find a single working handgun. Were we soon about to test his success that day?

Today Maya was wearing her normal spray on jeans and a pair of Topsiders with rawhide laces. I couldn't imagine where she'd come up with them. She could hardly have anticipated the coming river run when we were packing.

At my side, the harbormaster was rubbing his hands together. Suddenly his cell came out.

"Yes," Cody said. "Let's have Luis come over to talk about this. In case we agree, he ought to be ready to leave from here, because time matters. But I want you to know that we're not easy."

"Of course not! He will be ready to leave at your command, once you have paid his fee."

Twenty-five minutes later an open river cruiser cleared the fort and headed our way. The glossy blue paint and bright metal tie down fittings on the gunwales reminded me of a chicken bus. On the bow was the name *Malvina* in an elaborate script. I suppose the masculine form might have been *Malvino*, which loosely means bad wine. I didn't dwell on this. Under the white canvas canopy the pilot waved to us.

"It looks well kept," said Maya hopefully. She snapped a photo of it on her cell, as if to use it later in evidence. I wasn't feeling great about this sudden development, but the ferry was gone, and improvisation is a skill highly valued in the Agency for reasons we sometimes ended up questioning.

Luis tied up at the pier and Cody went over to talk to him. Our theory was that as the biggest person among us he would be the best negotiator. On the force he'd also had some training for hostage situations. I turned and glimpsed the harbormaster's face in the grimy window of his shack. He was certainly going to get a cut of this fee from Luis. I walked over and examined the boat. The interior was as freshly painted as the exterior. It looked like it had seating for ten passengers plus the pilot in the narrower stern. There was ample room for luggage, and I could see no damp spots in the bottom. The motor was a large outboard that looked like it had seen a lot of service, but if it had been as well maintained as the boat we'd be all right. It was about one-thirty and with a little luck we'd be in Livingston for dinner. This sounded good, but we'd left Antigua so quickly we didn't have any idea where we were going to stay that night. I assumed that being on the Caribbean, the town would have ample accommodations, especially since it was a bit past high season.

Cody walked back to us with a look of chagrin. "I think we're getting hit with gringo prices. He wants a thousand quetzales."

"A nice round number and about $135 US," I said. "Just make sure he's got a full tank of gas." This was in a country where most people make around the equivalent of five dollars a day in limp, well-used quetzales.

"His argument is that he doesn't have any fare coming back and it's a three and a half hour trip each way. He pointed out that it's not like the ferry that always has paying passengers in both directions."

"And he didn't say you were an American and you could damn well afford it," Maya added.

"But he thought it," I said.

"What would Bernard say if he were here?" Maya said. "It's his dime. That dear old guy." Was she now getting sentimental about Bernard? Cody caught my eye for a brief moment.

"Bernard would say 'Go for it. You're already there on the ground,'" I said, with what I felt was a good imitation of both his tone and his rhetoric.

And so we did.

CHAPTER FIFTEEN

To begin on a most difficult episode that followed our boarding the *Malvina*, the kind that nearly always happens after the deceptively easy period where little is happening, let me say first that Luis De Léon reminded me of Carlos Santana. In itself, that was in no way threatening, because I had always admired Santana as a musician. It was even a plus. Luis' lined face displayed a substantial mustache, and was topped by a small unserious reddish brown hat. His lively eyes were unserious as well. This is going to be a fun trip, they promised. Many fun things have been suggested to me in the past (witness the multiple invitations of Barbara Watt, potentially among the funnest), and so my attitude is usually wait and see. But there is always the lingering question: might what's coming be more fun for you and less fun for me?

With our luggage secured in the bow by simple gravity, we pulled away from the concrete pier in a confident manner, although I'm sure the Titanic made an even better display. The motor was noisy, but since we were moving off in a determined fashion toward an important destination, no one objected. Along the sides were hung more than enough life rings for all of us.

The current and the weather offered no challenge. The wake behind us feathered out benignly over quiet waters. Looking out into the clear, sunny estuary dotted with small islands, we were all quite certain that this would turn out to be no aquatic Guatemala City, although I had noticed Cody's gun still subtly bulging in his armpit. After an uneventful half hour, cruising far from shore on both sides, two conical islands came into view. Covered with tall trees, their branches were crowded with cormorants in one case, and pelicans in the next. They were like two adjacent neighborhoods that regarded each other with generations-old suspicion, although they both made their living in the same way.

Cody and Maya were both relaxed, and I had unwound a long way myself. I would've enjoyed having a conversation with Luis De Leon about the river and the marvelously complex eco-system we were observing, but the noise of the motor squelched any idea of conversation.

After nearly an hour he cut the speed by half and stepped forward with an announcement. "Here we are now passing through the lagoon. The legal requirements are that we go more slowly, to create fewer wakes, and not to disturb the wildlife. This will take about half an hour. Every boat has this rule, even the ferry that you missed."

Around us the small islands increased in number and length. Gnarled stands of mangrove gripped the shore. Between them wide ponds of water lilies floated placidly like green dinner plates. Long legged birds with wide feet walked over them harvesting a meal along their edges. The slower pace gave us an opportunity to talk.

"What is this place?" Cody said to Luis.

He shrugged as if fielding questions like this was the reason he deserved the higher fees we'd paid. "Why, this is the heart of the Río Dulce (sweet river). People think it is called that because the pressure of the outward flow from the great lake behind us keeps the salt water of the Caribbean from coming up this far. That in itself is true, as far as it goes, but even more it is that the birds and the animals of the river know this to be the finest place in all of Guatemala to live."

Further down, the lagoon widened to provide ample docking for some impressive watercraft, without alienating its bird life.

I'm no expert on pleasure boats, but some of the anchored yachts we were passing must have had multi-million dollar price tags. Near one palm-shadowed mansion with deeply overhanging eaves, a helicopter covered in tailored canvas was awaiting its owner's return. I began to get a greater sense of where the money was centered in Guatemala. This might be a neighborhood that housed the people who owned all the ATM machines. Possibly some of them also sold machine pistols and bulletproof vests to the security companies as a lucrative sideline. Eventually the long line of yachts ended and the jungle reclaimed the shoreline.

"I could easily live like that," Maya said wistfully.

"Not as a detective," Cody said. "Living like that depends most upon minding your own business." He must've felt strongly about that, because he rarely contradicted her.

As we cruised on through a narrower stretch in the stream Luis cut the motor even further. We were now putting along like an elderly tuc tuc. On the left was a long island populated by palms and thatched cottages. The walls were painted in vivid blues and reds. Tiny timber docks gave hopeful access to the river traffic, but not to a boat the size we were on. A few houses were even built on stilts at the shore. This may have been about land titles. Beyond, people moved about half concealed within the thick ground cover. We could hear distant rhythmic music. It was mainly the drumbeats that carried on the water that far out. The natives are restless, I thought, but I didn't want to say that. Again the scene took me right back to *The African Queen*. But I was no Bogart and Maya couldn't pass as Katharine Hepburn, although she shared some of that actress's forthright style.

From one of the makeshift docks a canoe abruptly pulled away. Two smallish people were paddling furiously toward us. I couldn't make out more than that, not even whether they were armed. Were they pigmies?

Seeing this too, Cody shook his head. "Dammit, I knew this would happen if we slowed down this much. Now the natives are coming after us. It's a good thing there are only two of them. I can hold them off once they get a little closer. Prepare to get down out of sight." He reached into his shirt and drew out the dreaded .45 automatic.

For some reason Luis snickered at our degree of preparedness. For me that ended any hope of a tip for him, even if we arrived in Livingston an hour early with a tuc tuc waiting at the dock. Clearly he had spent no time at all in Guatemala City. Why were we giving this man the big money? Was it only to set us up in some godforsaken backwater in eastern Guatemala? At least he hadn't billed himself as a guide, only as a river pilot. He knew the water, I told myself, but nothing more. I prepared myself to duck out of sight when the shooting began and gestured Maya to do the same.

Three minutes later, on closer view, it appeared that we were going to be boarded by two girls about nine and eleven years old. Taking no prisoners, they were armed with a pair of long paddles and a basket full of the local crafts. I'm used to being commercially assailed in plazas all over México, but attack me from a canoe on an obscure bend in a jungle river in Guatemala, and I'm your helpless prisoner. As they pulled up, with an experienced hand Luis threw them a rope and cut the engine. He knew this stretch of the Río Dulce quite well. Maybe he also knew his cut with these preteen mercenaries.

"So not everything is about crime here," Maya said. "It's more about where you are at the moment."

Cody leaned over in her direction. "I think at any given moment you're in a market. Don't ever forget that."

The canoe was a dugout formed from a single log. The girls offered a wide variety of shells, both loose and strung into necklaces and bracelets, a couple of coconuts, an assortment of woven palm leaf fans, and a dozen floral wreaths meant for headgear. I bought one for Maya for three quetzales.

We chatted briefly, but Cody signaled Luis it was time to move on, so he waved the girls off. I tried to imagine their remote island lifestyle. Did they even have cell phone service? If so, how did they pay for it? The rest of the world had abandoned the use of shells as money eons ago.

The motor came to life with a disturbing belch, as if something unrefined had been lurking in the gas. It purred neutrally for about a minute, then belched again with fading emphasis, and died. With a look of chagrin Luis removed part of the cowl and peered into the complicated hardware. The nuances of internal combustion engines are not my main area of expertise, and I turned away.

"I suppose you couldn't be out of gas so soon?" Maya said softly.

"We have more than half remaining. I know this."

Cody studied his watch. "It's coming up on three-thirty." The three of us eyed each other uneasily. Livingston seemed to be receding further out of reach as we sat there bobbing on the river. Soon the town would sink below the horizon entirely, and we still were not sure why we wanted to be there. Next night would fall. Luis swore softly, groped beneath his seat, and came up with a small collection of tools in an ancient, thoroughly scarred cigar box. *Romeo y Julieta* read the cover, now secured along the back edge with the broad silvery fabric outline of what could only be a strip of American duct tape.

Excited birdcalls expanded around us in both number and volume, as if the *Malvina* had now been spotted as a cargo of promising carrion even if it was still showing a few signs of life. With a look of deepening disgust, Maya yanked off her bridal wreath and spun it into the water like a vengeful Frisbee. From below, something eager lunged at the floral edges, then backed away. Who knew piranha could appear this far north?

"Not to worry anymore on this emergency journey," said Luis in an offhand tone, showing too many smiling teeth as he waved our concerns away with a free hand. "I can simply back off the fuel line and then reconnect it. You soon will see, since I have done this before."

How many times? I thought.

He started to unscrew a connection between the gas tank and the underside of the motor. When it came free at both ends, acrid flammable fumes filled the boat. We all pinched our noses as he placed one end to his lips and blew hard. As his cheeks expanded like trial balloons, something pale in color like a gob of chicken fat flew in an arc out of the other end into the water. It lingered on the surface for a few seconds, than sank in a way that healthy fat never does. Nothing went for it, even though a small, multicolored iridescent ring remained on the surface to mark its watery disappearance.

Nodding with a reassuring grin, Luis hummed as he reconnected the fuel line.

As the master of a few obscure skills myself, I'm always quick to grant others some degree of latitude in their area of expertise. But when Luis' restart process, repeated several times, yielded nothing more from the engine, not even a hiccup, his stock took a major hit. His response was to again start diddling the small parts under the cowl. One glance at Maya told me she was now for the third time counting the life rings hanging on the gunwales. She had long ago written off the idea of getting to Livingston that evening.

Cody leaned over toward Luis in a forceful way. Understandably, Luis leaned away from that deepening shadow in the stern. "Now is not the time to fuck with us," Cody said with a kindly smile. "Get some help out here right away. This is an issue bigger than this boat, or even your life. You've got a cell in your back pocket. Just use it, now!"

Don't we all now and then like to put on a brave front when it's called for? I can't say I had ever seen Cody do it, because his level of experience didn't require that kind of pretense, but that was what was happening now. Maya flashed him a confident grin.

"Now he is between the sword and the wall," she whispered so that only the two of us could hear.

With an ugly look, Luis punched in a number on his cell, which appeared to work better than his boat motor. He placed his hand over his mouth as he spoke.

Cody rose. "Do you need the coordinates of this location?" he said.

Luis waved him off. "I have them."

So technology was still alive on the obscure bayous of the Río Dulce.

And so were we, but our case was on life support.

CHAPTER SIXTEEN

Much of the planet's third world population probably sleeps on straw. In San Miguel, there is a project that collects the universally dispensed plastic bags and makes them into mattresses for the poor. That night, sleeping in a thatched hut on our two-acre island, we fell short on both systems. Dirt is hard to sleep on, even when you have a nasty layer of worn-out canvas between you and the soil.

Although I can always vouch for the accuracy of the Agency's cost-keeping records for our clients, I awakened wanting to charge Bernard Emerson far more than the ten quetzales we paid for our collective lodging that night. At about forty-four cents American per bed I felt he was getting off way too easy when we hadn't, even though our landlord was clearly planning a shindig with his unexpected windfall. He had cheerfully spent the night under the trees with his wife and two young daughters.

Of course there's no need for a shower when you

have the Río Dulce practically at your doorstep. During some part of the year, it was probably also inside your doorstep. Maya struggled to collect her hair into a manageable mass as we stumbled to the shoreline, only to find Cody there before us counting his bones with his probing fingertips. We had also brought our bathing suits and we plunged in.

"I now know where every single one of my ribs is," he said. "At least they're all there, I think. Even some I didn't remember in this kind of detail."

These are the consolations of remote jungle travel in this technologically advanced era. Luis may have gone to a more receptive welcoming, or at least one more familiar with his shortfalls, but by what means? Was it by one of those girl-driven canoes? Their system looked better than ours at that moment. People who are more technologically sophisticated than I am say that having fewer working parts makes for greater reliability. Some call this *elegance*. Although his boat had been towed in and tied up at a shaky wooden dock that was no less chancy than his progress down the river, Luis had offered us no refunds, thinking perhaps as he escaped, that we would make it up on the cheap lodging costs. It is at times like this that I struggle to keep from generalizing.

Of course I'm making these notes more than a month later, among all the comforts of our home on Calle Quebrada in San Miguel, so I know how this ends, and it's not pretty. But that morning on the Río Dulce it also looked as bleak as any case we'd had, so we weren't disillusioned by the resolution as it fell out several days later. Our mosquito bites have long since healed, of course, and that unpleasant brownish tropical fungus that had started up on my left middle toe is only partly healed but shrinking in area every day. I believe that soon Maya will let me return from the guest bedroom. She's always quite delicate about her skin, but I guess we all must bear the scars of our best efforts, even if we have to do so alone. She came away from our Guatemala excursion remarkably intact, not something everyone in this fracas could say.

We never did form a clear impression of our hosts. Were they the parents of our aquatic craft sellers? After the modest exchange of quetzales, which they examined carefully for the watermark, they had retreated into the bush, as if any further hospitality services were beyond their capability or understanding. Although none of our party had died, I began to appreciate the concept of refugee much better. After our al fresco bathing, a careful morning walk around the island suggested we were alone, a disconcerting thought. It was many years since I had read *Robinson Crusoe*, but the few memories I had of it were not reassuring. Fortunately this snafu had not happened on a Friday. Our single gun had never been sufficiently reassuring. We had three cell phones among us, but no idea who to call. Siri seemed mute on our situation, and the Google street maps app was frankly baffled by our location. Technology is not helpful when there is no one on the other side to bounce your hopeful signals back.

We did still have all our luggage, and at about eleven o'clock that morning when a boat similar to that of Luis pulled up at our 'pier', we crowded around to shake the pilot's hand. Maya stood behind me counting out our remaining quetzales. We needed all of them and seventy-eight U.S. dollars more to book our fares into Livingston, where we pulled up at a substantial if well-used pier in time for a one-thirty lunch. Our new boat for half a trip had cost the same as the first one.

That last part of the journey had been uneventful beyond the motor noise. But it was better than no motor noise. The boat was reliable and so was the motor. The pilot, whose name we never heard (but we suspected was probably Luis) had little to say, keeping his dour gaze fixed on a point beyond the bow, as if he already knew our doubtful history and didn't want to get involved. By that point in our travels I could easily understand why. We may have given off an aura of the albatross, never a good omen for water travellers.

The Río Dulce broadened out into a bay near the end. We had seen no more islands, and the waves were shallow but rolling in continuously from the sea beyond. Since the color was now a dull silvery blue, I felt we had entered deeper water, loosing that muddier cast of the Dulce behind us. The sun was blazing and unfriendly. In that broader mouth of the river the shore was dotted with small settlements, and we hugged the northern beach. It had the height of a promontory perhaps thirty meters above the water. Vaguely off to the southeast was an urban mound of some importance, probably Puerto Barrios, but from that perspective, it was lacking any detail.

And then we arrived. Luis the second looked away in silence as we rose and cheered. Cody stepped authoritatively from a bench seat over the gunwale onto the concrete pier and offered a hand first to Maya and then to me. Our pilot pulled off the luggage and sped away without another word. This felt rude for Guatemala, and for any place in Latin America, but we had landed. Up a serpentine slope under the palms was the Villa Caribe, a place we had never heard of. Our current goal was to make it our home. To shower with soap but without bathing suits, to sleep on a real mattress, and to drink hot coffee in the morning was our collective dream.

The hotel staff rushed out to help bring up our luggage. If by their attitude they seemed to suggest we were the first guests that they'd had in a while, that only seemed right to a trio of weary and frustrated travelers, even if it wasn't true. We were able to shift from survival to investigation mode in short order, after a big lunch and a glass or two of chilled white wine.

By three o'clock we were walking about Livingston with a more relaxed step than we'd had anywhere in some time. We were all testing our powers of observation. Twenty years earlier, I had spent a couple of weeks in the Bahamas and a few days in Barbados, and this town strongly reminded me of those porch-fronted houses, the bold creative color palette, the unapologetic laid back native lifestyle. The people on the street were all black or probably mixed black and Hispanic, all with a dash of the indigenous Caribe people. I didn't see any tourists, but we didn't seem to stand out in people's reaction when they noticed us. It didn't take long before we were all saying to ourselves, "Why would Darren Hall and Barbara Watt want to end up here?" Was there an anthropological aspect to the mixing of cultures that had drawn Darren Hall this far east?

The street dogs presented a wretched story. They were lounging everywhere in the dusty unpaved streets, afflicted with mange and patchy fur, missing or stiffened limbs, thin to the point of being walking skeletons. They were largely indifferent to the sparse rattling traffic of the tuc tucs, which made them more vulnerable. I've often thought of dogs as perennially hopeful, but this group displayed as little optimism as any I'd ever seen. To survive in Livingston would require starting a dog ranch for the old and the needy.

We stopped at a busy looking restaurant called Las Tres Garifunas. It displayed a thatched roof and a wooden salmon-colored façade. Maya went in bearing Darren and Ixobel's photo and an optimistic look. She was seeking two lost friends. Had they come this way? Two minutes later she came out shaking her head.

"What?" Cody said. "Did they hassle you?"

She shrugged. "No. They offered me a job as a waitress. It didn't pay as well as the Agency, even with tips. And they didn't recognize either Darren or Ixobel."

"But this is not the end of the road," Cody said. "We just need to settle in and develop a strategy for tomorrow. We've been so delayed already, I don't think one more day will matter much."

We paced off the narrow limits of Livingston, taking note of the major landmarks (none), cross streets (four), shady places to stop and wipe our brows (nineteen). We inquired at three more restaurants with the same zero result. If Darren was there, he was either keeping a low profile or he always ate at home. I wondered for a moment if he was even still alive. And if Barbara Watt was there she had to be wearing a burka to conceal her pale skin and blazing blond hair. As the afternoon wound down our only success was finding a larcenous ATM on the outer wall of a closed bank that gave us enough quetzales to go on, for a fee that made Maya stutter. But at least no one mugged us as we moved off with a replenished purse.

At five-thirty we reconvened in the deeply shaded restaurant bar in the Villa Caribe. Overhead, most of the palm trees were real. The ones directly over the bar looked chancy, but I suppose that fake ones don't shed. Walking in we'd been able to take a greater interest in the architecture. The hotel was a long white two-story structure that followed the ridge along the bay. It could easily have offered sixty or seventy rooms. If Humphrey Bogart had never slept there in one of his tropical efforts, he should have. Here, framed in an early 1940s ambience, faded elegance met touches of tropical seediness, and it still worked, since I now felt we'd come to earth in a real place. In fact I was reminded of the retro impression I'd had reading Bernard Emerson's original query back in San Miguel. *"You don't know me, Mr. Zacher."* That letter had begun this adventure. Why did I feel were we all somewhat naive then? Would the case now wind down in this Garifuna backwater town on the steamy Caribbean?

Without raising that issue to the others, I was guessing that we were all rather hoping it would. This case had more miles piled up on the front end of it than any we'd ever taken on.

The bar was situated so that patrons could sit either inside or out. One part was not cooler than the other. We took a table with a view over the piers.

When a waiter came over to take our order I asked him a question.

"We've been walking all around Livingston and I haven't seen any hotel nearly as inviting as this one. Is it the only one of its kind in town? It seems like no one would want to stay anywhere else."

"Of course," he said smugly. Maya was already fishing in her purse to find the photo of Darren.

"We had some friends staying in town recently," Cody said, cordially. "I wonder if they stayed here? I believe they're kind of fussy about their accommodations."

Maya slid the Darren and Ixobel photo across the table. The waiter leaned over without picking it up, then after a moment shook his head. "No, I haven't seen either of them here. I would remember that red hair."

"Where else would they have stayed then?" I said.

With a sigh, his stature increased by a couple of centimeters. "There is nowhere else, at least like this. That's why the ferry lands at our pier. Perhaps your friends stayed with relatives, although they don't look much like we do here. I just don't know. So what will we be having today?"

We gave him our order. It included some snacks but not dinner, since we weren't that hungry after a late lunch. He started to pile up our menus.

"I just have one more question. There is a woman that might also have been trying to meet with them. I wish I had her photo, but I don't." If I had been carrying around Barbara's photo Maya would've strangled me as I slept. "I can describe her this way. About thirty years old, tall like an American, which she is, with bright blond hair and beautiful to look at. Striking, in fact. Yet, her Spanish is like she was born speaking it."

A knowing smile overtook our server. "Naturally we all remember her here from only the two days of her stay, and her wonderful *propinas* (tips). We call her *la güera*, the blonde. No one in the hotel remembers seeing anyone like her before."

"Duh," said Maya, working the cutting edge of her American slang lexicon.

"But she is no longer staying here?" Cody added. "We're sad to hear that."

"So are we. But also she left for us no forwarding address. And, if I may say so with no rudeness, she departed very quickly, and in the night. You can imagine how it can be difficult to get a tuc tuc at four o'clock in the morning."

"Did someone come to pick her up? Maybe she didn't need to try." I could hardly imagine her leaving any other way.

Our waiter shrugged. "I was not on duty then, so this is only what I have heard."

"When was this?"

"Two nights ago." While his left hand gripped the

menus, his right hand lingered open at the palm along the edge of the table. Knowing he would be embarrassed to be an informant, Maya slid a fifty-quetzal note into it without looking at him. I could see her entering the expenditure of $6.75 U.S. later in her Emerson expense journal.

Thrusting the note into his pocket, the waiter hastened away with our order. We had learned little about our goal, but more about the chase. That was more than we had recently been getting.

"I wonder what that was about?" I said, "Barbara leaving in the middle of the night like that."

Maya gave me a frank look. "Obviously she had run into someone who looked just like you."

I shrugged that off. "But it makes me wonder where she's staying now, if this is the only suitable hostelry in town. I think in the morning we'll have to make some low key enquiries about important homes here."

"Especially the ones with posh guestrooms," Cody said.

CHAPTER SEVENTEEN

Maybe it was true that Barbara ran off with someone who looked like me, but I doubt it. Barbara was no less on a mission than we were, and it wasn't about me. We had a couple more glasses of wine with no conversation of any substance, and adjourned to our rooms. Maya and I were both ready to go to bed, and I'm sure Cody was too. Our forty-four-cent dirt floor accommodations of the previous night needed to be erased in our recollections. Under my watch, I wasn't sure they would even make it into our notes when it was time to write up this case. While Maya and I often had lengthy conversations in bed about the current venture, that night, sleep was more compelling. It felt wonderful to be in a real bed.

Our main floor room had a wide view of the harbor, with the facing wall made of a series of jalousie blinds that opened or closed on a lever. We could also walk through a door in the center and sit on a small patio. The inside was screened to keep out nocturnal bugs. If the furniture was rather well used, it was also graced with a distinctly tropical character, with a creative use of bamboo and exotic jungle woods. In contrast, the tile floor and the painted walls were quite fresh. If we didn't know much more about why we were spending the night in Livingston, it didn't matter. Nothing could disturb our blissful rest, or so we thought.

At twelve forty-seven the following morning a charismatic bolt of lightning seared the inside of our eyelids, and four seconds later the explosive thunder shattered our hearing. Maya and I nearly collided leaping out of bed. But that was merely an anthem for the symphonic downpour that followed in less than a minute. Maya and I had never had a conversation on the subject of rain, but growing up in southeastern Ohio I felt I knew something about it. Maya had always lived in the drier climates of central México. While the weather could occasionally turn on you in both places, rarely did it so thoroughly obliterate your faith in Nature as a benign spirit.

This was tropical violence, more than mere rain. With the wind howling behind it, I was sure boats were going down that night. We were in no way prepared for it, and I'm not sure there is an English word that could adequately describe it. The nuance of the Spanish word, *tormenta*, is good, but while it sounds evil, it only means a storm. This was the kind of downpour that would've stifled the early volcanoes in the dinosaur era. In trying to understand this, Maya and I soon realized that our survival skills were at the elementary school level. We've all seen rather frivolous photos of American Cold War school kids cringing under their desks in rehearsals for surviving a nuclear attack. Rain in San Miguel sometimes offers a close equivalent in frivolity, leaving tiny puddles in the low spots of the patio pavers at our house on Quebrada. I once saw some pea-sized hail that made a few extra holes in the leaves of the split leaf philodendrons. Rarely, rain ran freely in the streets of centro, but it was still nothing like this.

This was a level of rain that provided little room for air spaces between the drops. Once I was awake enough to grasp what we were hearing and seeing, my first thought was to wonder how a substance as thin and unsubstantial as air could hold and then release the shear weight of tens of thousands of tons of almost continuous, uninterrupted masses of water.

"When we left San Miguel you thought snake-proof shorts were the key to survival on this case," I said, spitting out the words between thunderous outbursts. "But now we know it's really going to take scuba gear to make it out of here." Maya's only response was to slide closer to me and take my hand in both of hers. Naturally, by then we had completely sealed our room (as we thought), by cranking down the handles of the glass blinds that kept the torrential beast from getting its teeth further into us. But they still streamed leakage in response. This rain was not merely falling that night in Livingston, it was driven. Noah must've been awakened in this same way.

In the Paul Zacher Agency all of us hate luck. We'd had a terribly violent case a couple of years ago that we filed as *Identity Crisis*, where our collective survival hinged on luck going our way. Nothing else could've saved us. We took an oath later that we never wanted to survive in that fashion again, since luck was too unpredictable to use as an asset. Wasn't this outburst of a hostile nature an example to take home of what happens when luck doesn't work?

In the morning that Garifuna world seemed bruised and damaged when I peered out through the still streaming glass blinds. Broken off palm fronds littered the ground. The tall grass had been flattened. Whole coconuts lay about that had not shattered on impact. I could see now why the trees had such flexible trunks. It made me wonder how disasters like this would affect the local people's worldview. They had seemed cheerful enough when we saw them on the streets the evening before. Were they just smarter than anyone else, and more experienced? Our history suggested we'd been through a record-breaking event.

Maya and I composed ourselves for breakfast like two of the privileged few who had scrambled onto the Titanic lifeboats in good time. Of course, that kind of thinking always left you wondering about the ones that hadn't. We found we didn't have much to say to each other about last night. You can't generalize easily about a unique event.

The waiter who came up seemed surprisingly fresh and untroubled about what he must've been through too, unless he lived in a weatherproof bunker. These were tougher people than I thought.

"How can I serve you this morning?"

Maya gave him a frank look, which she usually didn't waste on staff people. "You look like you survived that quite well."

He glanced down at his uniform, which was composed of creased black slacks and a white shirt under a black vest. It wasn't perfectly clean, but it would do after everything we'd all been through. I was surprised that he was still able to look that good. He evidently wasn't.

"You're not even wet," I said, in a kindly manner, I thought.

"Last night was nothing new, if that's what you're talking about," he said, looking at us as newbies. "We've had only two like it this week, so far."

We both looked at him for a long moment. "Don't tell me that's normal," I said.

"Then don't ask, because it was. We get sixty or seventy nights like that every year. Three in one week isn't unusual. You get used to it. I guess four in a week would be too much."

Maya and I both nodded in silence as he moved away with our order. "What a lucky place to live," she said after he was out of earshot. "To get dumped on like that all the time."

"For underwear you would use a bathing suit here, that's all. No umbrella ever made is going to save you."

She looked at me solemnly. "Paul, I know you think you're kidding, but I have one along that's perfect for this weather."

Of course she did, and it would probably match her Topsiders.

Unless you're loaded down with luggage, you don't need a tuc tuc to find your way around Livingston, but nonetheless that three-wheeler vehicle suggested a strategy for us to find either the *güera* (Barbara Watt), or Darren Hall and Ixobel, whether together or apart. We hadn't seen Cody at breakfast, but there are times when Maya and I like to run off by our own, as she likes to say, and in the past that has led to several delightful outcomes. Neither of us had any confidence that it always did, but what else did we have going? Detective work, as we've learned is mostly waiting, sifting through piles of irrelevant 'evidence,' and talking over what we think we know.

At ten-thirty of the morning after the storm, under a blazing sky, we appeared on the blacktop driveway of our hotel, bearing the tentative look of tourists from anywhere. For this outing I had worn a pair of Madras plaid Bermuda shorts, an outfit no informed adult male would ever wear in Latin America, but I hate to throw away items of clothing from my best days of college, especially when at forty I can still get into some of them, even when it makes Maya queasy. Emerging onto the street I was surprised to see a few cars, and even an ambulance parked a block down. There must be a regular ferry now that the road to Puerto Barrios was closed, possibly even going as far back upriver as San Felipe de Lara. It made me wonder how our rental car was doing, our Nissan Maxima. Was it up on blocks now with all the wheels missing and two families living inside? It was insured.

Maya spotted a tuc tuc ahead. I held a single page town map in my hand that the front desk had graciously furnished to us, not realizing it was no more than a cheap prop to convince the driver we were average tourists, a little confused, a little apprehensive, and more than a little lost. Our next interrogation was less than four minutes off.

"Please do not show your money to people on the street when you pay me," the driver said when we climbed into the next waiting tuc tuc. This earned our confidence immediately, which may have been why he said it. He didn't seem macho enough himself to try to seize our money.

"And don't you show yours when you give us change," I said back at him. "We're not here about money, but we do know how important it is to be careful."

"So you are here today thinking about people using drugs as seen on the TV?" He looked through the mirror into my lower face. "Perhaps you would like to find some for yourselves. I know a way."

"Not even close," barked Maya. "You will need to listen carefully to what we're going to tell you, and get your priorities in order," she said.

I confess that I liked this new authoritative side of Maya. Even when she had absorbed it from Mexican movies and you knew it came from a series of heroines that usually ended up paying for their boldness.

"At your service," the man said in an undertone. I couldn't get a good look at his face, but he was middle aged and wearing a colorful do-rag that suggested a Caribbean musician on his day off. There are worse looks, particularly in that part of the world.

"Do you ever work in the small hours of the night?" Maya said.

"I do when there's a special need for it, but it costs extra. What are you thinking? Do you need to be picked up from a bar?"

"I don't want it for myself," Maya said. "We had a friend who left the hotel two nights ago at four in the morning. She was an attractive blonde and she may have needed a little protection. I was thinking she might have used two drivers."

The driver thought for a moment. "You are offering to pay for this information today? I mean, we are not just having a friendly conversation?"

"If it's at a reasonable price," I said, "and I hope it's still friendly. We are not wealthy people, but we do need to find our friend, and quickly." We had not specified a destination when we got in, but we were nonetheless moving at a crawl through town. We might have been part of a funeral procession. The dogs lying in the street barely bothered to look up at us as we passed. One did and rolled his only eye.

"Although I was not there when the blond woman left that night, I have heard some things, OK? The other drivers will talk, since most of the time this job is not very interesting. It will cost two hundred quetzales." About $27 U.S., which might be worth it if the information was genuine. There was rarely any way to tell until afterward, and not always then.

"I have one more thing that might help you

remember, because this is a photo of two people who may have been with her that night. We are not sure, but it is possible." Maya reached into her travel purse and drew out the Darren and Ixobel photo that was now growing frayed around the edges and dog-eared at the corners. As the driver turned to take it, another small paper that had come out of her purse behind it fluttered to the bare metal floor. Reflexively he captured it in his fingers without losing sight of the street.

He looked first at the photo. "Well, no. I do not know them. As for this..." he paused to open the retrieved paper, which had been folded into four segments to the size of a matchbook. Over his shoulder I saw it was the logo part of a letterhead that Luis Figueroa had snipped from some correspondence at our meeting at the Banco Comercial in Guatemala City. While it had seemed reasonable to bring it along, we'd never found any use for it. There on the front was the ornately embellished M that had held no meaning for any of us at the time. Aside from the fact that it must belong to someone Darren was doing business with, we had largely stopped thinking about it.

The driver thrust the paper and the photo back over his shoulder with a muffled gasp. "You will get out of my tuc tuc now," he said in a painful tone. "I can tell you nothing else, but only this: you must leave Livingston without delay."

Ten seconds later Maya and I were left standing on the sidewalk as the tuc tuc sped away fast enough to raise a cloud of dust. We blankly studied the M for a moment.

"Is it for Henry Morgan?" I said after a while. "He was a seventeenth century pirate who plagued the Spanish holdings in this area."

"But would his name still inspire that kind of reaction?"

"I wonder if the scrollwork around the M might be stylized hemp leaves," I said, holding it closer to my eyes and wishing we had a magnifying glass.

Five minutes later another tuc tuc came by. Maya flagged it down. "We might as well talk to as many drivers as we can before they all figure out what we're up to. I wish I knew."

We settled in the back and the driver turned. "We would like to see how the rich people live here," Maya said, fanning her face with one hand. Initially this brought her a blank look.

Finally he said, "What does rich mean to you? We have a few people who do better than most, but would they be rich to someone from Río or Buenos Aires? I don't think so."

"I'm from Mexico City. Rich there means people who can buy their house for cash." This was a good way to say it, because mortgages were rare in México. They were most often found attached to government housing projects or gated developments trying to get launched. The interest rates were rarely survivable.

"Well, there is one street, and it's very short. We can go there. I show you."

I knew Maya was thinking that Barbara wouldn't have departed the hotel in the middle of the night to end up staying in one of the ramshackle buildings around us. We had parked in front of the Happy Fish Restaurant. Someone in the hotel had recommended it, but it would never have been Barbara Watt's style to dine there.

With a sputter that reminded me too well of our river cruise, we drove off past the Río Dulce Juice Bar and turned right a block further onto a narrower paved street. The first establishment was an AA meeting place on the left called la Esperanza, *hope*. I felt like stopping in. Sober as we were, we also needed a little hope now too, but the driver kept on going.

Two blocks down we slowed from a trot to a crawl. It was a block of the same style of housing, two story wood frame houses with picket fences fronting broad porches and a scattering of steamboat gothic detail. Here the paint colors had been as naively chosen as on the main street. Sometimes they worked. The main difference was that we saw more smiling faces. The owners really were doing better there than their neighbors who were living closer to or on the commercial strip.

Maya and I looked at each other. It was time to play our hole card. We didn't bother with the Barbara description this time. Maya pulled out the Darren Hall photo. I could see she again had the letterhead logo folded beneath it, this time on purpose. She handed it to him with more than a hint of her old seductive glance. "Tell me everything you know," her manner said, "and I will whisper my own secrets in your ear."

Who knew how many times that had worked for her before she met me? I frankly didn't want to speculate.

The tuc tuc driver surveyed the Darren Hall photo with little interest, until he pulled it closer. "This woman, I think I have taken her to places more than one time. Those square glasses she wears, do you know?"

"Do you recall where you took her?" Maya said.

Surely our driver's shrug was not up to the pure Mexican standard, but why should it be? It mostly expressed a reluctance to accept personal responsibility, while the Mexican version rejected outright the undisclosed plan of those corrupt tycoons who ran the universe. I realize these are merely cultural differences, but I'm always trying to read them.

"There is another sheet under that photo," Maya reminded him.

The driver glanced at her briefly as he pulled it over the photo.

"God in Heaven! I am a Protestant, as you can

see, but I still would not ever deal with this man."

"Then tell me his name," she said softly, showing no fear, "so I can avoid him too," She could often do this better than I did.

The driver looked at her as if she might not be ready for the information she had requested. He scanned the street all around us before he spoke. "You will never say how you know this?"

She looked at him solemnly. "I would sacrifice my virginity first!"

This was a statement I had not heard Maya use before, and with quite good reason. Perhaps Guatemala offered less skepticism in this area. Naturally she couldn't look at me as she said it. The driver leaned toward both of us and placed his hand over his mouth.

"It is the mark of the Merchant that you now have in your hand. Few here would allow themselves to touch this."

"There are many merchants here as elsewhere," I offered, as always looking for more detail. In art as in life, it's the detail that brings the painting alive.

"I mean Lionel Merchant. Now I must ask you to leave my tuc tuc here. Say no more if you value the lives of my family and your own."

Maya placed a fifty-quetzal note in his hand and we watched as he sped back up the street.

CHAPTER EIGHTEEN

After that breakthrough, the rest of the morning didn't offer much progress. Another tuc tuc ride had yielded no comment from the driver regarding either the photo or the logo. It cost more than the others because we weren't asked to leave as soon as the photo and the logo came out. When it ended I reached Cody's cell and we met for lunch at the Dugu Bar, a bright yellow frame cottage situated at the end of the paved footpath that led along the ridge to the hotel. It faced the street and one end overlooked an assortment of palms and flowering trees, punctuated by several electric poles festooned with clusters of wires and white can-like transformers. This was the road that led down to the beach.

The sign at the door read DRINK,s FOOD, TV & MUSIC. That was clear enough. I don't mind a little creative punctuation. The lettering was distributed over the beaming face of Bob Marley.

Maya and I settled at a table at the end of the

porch. "I suppose you already know what Dugu means," I said, thinking it was probably a traditional local stew with a seafood base, a house specialty in this area. She always did more research than Cody and I did.

"Of course, I looked it up online. It's a kind of extended funeral ceremony that's supposed to bring the dead person together with his relatives and ancestors."

"I hope that's not an omen."

Cody joined us a moment later. "First of all, I need a tall cold one just to be able to speak," he said. Sweat was already collecting on his brow. The waiter came out and we ordered two Mozas and a lemonade for Maya, who typically didn't drink beer. They offered a pulled pork sandwich that looked promising and we also ordered a round of those. We watched the street in silence for a while. After the waiter brought our drink order Cody drew off about half his glass. "I think we've got a problem here."

"I agree," I said. "We don't know where our victim is, or his two lovely associates."

"There is that, of course, but what I'm getting at here is that there is some kind of kingpin in charge behind the scenes in this town. It's about drugs, I think."

"A lot of things are," Maya said, sipping her lemonade delicately.

"What have you got?"

"Well, I spent the morning walking all around

this town. Before eleven o'clock I was hit up twice with offers to sell me a bag of weed. And that was on the main street. Both kids had the bag with them."

"How much?" I said, recalling prices for the Jamaica variety of grass when I was in college. There was also Panama red. The growing conditions in those places would probably yield the same kind of grass people grew here.

"A hundred fifty Q, so about twenty bucks."

"Did you get some papers too?" Maya said. "I know where I can get a lighter."

I waved this off, knowing she didn't mean it. "Prices haven't changed that much in twenty years," I said. "I was paying that as a junior in art school in Ohio."

"Here's a thing. I handled both of those bags to compare them, and they could've been brother and sister. Same heft—I couldn't actually weigh them, of course—but both were in an identical plastic bag, and the weed itself had the same buds and flowers, I swear. I handled a lot of that stuff when I was a cop, even working homicide."

"So, therefore it must come from the same source? Isn't that too small for a sample?" Maya said, never an easy sell.

This time Cody shrugged. "One more aspect of this is that sales territories for drugs tend to be under the control of one person or a single organization. That's why at home in México the turf is so bloody. There's always a lot of conflict at the edges. It's like trench warfare, and the front lines move back and forth. People die when they do. The American press is always there to count the bodies. Anyway, the two offers I had came at opposite ends of town. I think that means there's only one dealer in play here."

"Great job, " Maya said. As the head of the Agency it was her role to say this.

"Thank you. The only thing I couldn't determine was who was at the head of this organization. Who was giving orders?"

"And does that person connect to Darren Hall?" Maya said.

"Once again, who can say? But when you're talking about money and power, and as we walk around this town there's little of either in view, at least at the street level, why the hell not? Let's try to think who the players might be." He finished his beer at a gulp and turned around to locate the waiter.

"Exactly," said Maya, pulling out the photo and the logo once again. When Cody turned back to face us he couldn't avoid them.

"Of course I know the photo of Darrel and Ixobel, but this logo not so much. Did you get any response from showing it around?"

Maya leaned back in her wicker chair. "Yes we

did. I think the man at the head of your organization is named Lionel Merchant. He is a great power in this town, but behind the scenes, as you suggest. He is almost certainly the supplier of your street weed, and probably much more."

"Did you get a sense of how people feel about him?"

"Yes, they're petrified of him," she said. The sandwiches came and we chewed on them for a while, and also on the potential value of the new information.

"I'm trying without success to make a connection between drugs and Darren Hall," I said. "We've come up with nothing to suggest there was any before. Maybe there really is none. We didn't see anything in his house to suggest it."

"Maybe if we had gotten into his safe," Cody said, munching.

"What is Darren really doing?" Maya said. "I spent some time online looking for any kind of publication of his, anything at all. It's like he's invisible to the rest of the world. How can he survive like that, with no presence? As an anthropologist he must try to publish something now and then."

"It can only be that he prefers to have no visible presence," I said. "It suits his business style. He's operating in shadow, and his trade is underground."

"What a perfect fit for doing business with

Lionel Merchant," Maya said brightly, punching his name into the Internet on her cell, but soon shaking her head. "Nothing we could use for this. Of course the name is not unique. I can see a couple more here that don't fit."

I already knew there were a few other Paul Zachers. Hopefully none of them were also painters. Cody and I ordered two more Mozas when the waiter came by and cleared our dishes.

"You're in business," Cody said.

"Of course. Anyone in the arts is, aside from our Agency activities. If you're not in business then you're a hobbyist."

"And you're in the retail end of things."

"Sure. If you're wholesaling paintings, then you're a manufacturer, not a painter."

"I think I want to go into business for myself," Cody said. "Maybe it's too late." He had recently turned sixty.

"Then put away your gun. There are better means of promotion. What kind of business are you thinking of?"

"Drug distribution at the street level, but not here."

"Chicago is a tough town," I said, "but it might be a better place to start."

"That's where the money is," Maya said. "But not in quetzales. Paul sells his pictures for three and four thousand dollars, but I always thought the real money is with people who sell their product for a dollar or two. It's all about volume, not price."

I gave her a sharp look, not that she was wrong. "Lionel Merchant," I said. "Why don't we take him down, and see what four-legged creatures run away from the debris. Maybe it will be a door opening for us."

"Or two-legged creatures," said Maya. "Maybe one of them will be Darren Hall."

"I'm sure you're not the first one to say that, Paul," said Cody. "But I hope you're the last. If we start it and we don't succeed, we're probably not going to walk away from here."

A lot of our Zacher Agency gambles were based on coming in last, just in time to carry away the bodies when they could still tell us something more useful than they'd been willing to do in life. Like why they'd ended up in the path of a bullet.

We ordered another round of beers and lemonade and Cody told us about his idea for a new business venture, and how it wouldn't interfere with the Agency, and might even stimulate it.

CHAPTER NINETEEN

One thing I've noticed in this detective trade is that a lot of machismo is no more than bluff, and the kind of reaction Maya and I had seen in two of the tuc tuc drivers is the precise reaction machismo is designed to promote. Making your reputation as nasty as possible can bring about considerable savings in the cost of hired muscle, for example. I had to wonder whether this wasn't what we were seeing in Lionel Merchant's persona. We had no history on the man, and weren't likely to get any when people were so scared of talking about him, but this is the kind of public image you have when you've been around a long time and most people knew enough to not get any closer than they had to. The bottom line was that we still only had one gun, so how big a staff did he have? There had to be a way to find out.

Without protest, Maya walked back the hundred meters to the hotel after lunch. Armed or not, the violent parts of this business were never her preference. She would never talk about the two people she'd killed on earlier cases. I had a genuine fear that if she had to kill anyone else, she'd leave again, as she had once before, on our fourth case.

Cody had brought along his gun under a big shirt and, following his new plan, we hired a tuc tuc outside the Dugu Bar to see if we could scare up some trouble. A lot of times this business is about no more than getting in people's faces and watching how they react. If they feel threatened enough they'll often make mistakes.

The driver was not one we recognized. He was barely twenty. I wished I had my own gun, but it might be that like Lionel Merchant, we could use bravado to put on a bigger show than we could actually support with a field of fire. You never know about these things until you try it, or until you're hauled away on a gurney.

"I feel like having some fun today," Cody said, leaning forward over the driver's shoulder.

"This whole town is so much fun you do not believe it. What kind you need? Good time girls? Black Garifuna all you want and a few Chinese too, although they probably still sleeping this time of day." He looked at his watch. It was just a little after two.

"Maybe later. Right now I could use some good time weed to get me ready. The best." This conversation was carried on in English.

"Sure. I get you a bag very quick now. How big?

You get the papers in the drugstore, then he call the street boy."

That's why they call them drugstores, I thought. A block later we pulled up in front of la Farmacia Mil Sueños, the Thousand Dreams Drugstore. It was another typical two-story frame building, painted in red, orange, and blue, with a welcoming front porch offering two worn wicker sofas.

"I want fifty grams," Cody said. A little less than two ounces.

"Sure, you got it pronto. I need the cash first, three hundred Q. You won't need to worry about me running off somewhere." He slapped the keys to the tuc tuc into Cody's hand, which surprised both of us as he walked inside.

The papers came out in a minute or so, the classic Zig-Zags in a small blue plastic bag with a box of wooden matches. The driver nodded reassuringly as he got back in, but Cody didn't give him back his keys. We waited for eight or nine minutes until a kid in a tie-dyed tee shirt came up on a bicycle. It was not an ancient Schwinn with a basket on the front and balloon tires, but a Raleigh with pencil thin tires. It had to be forty years old. He was wearing a small violet school backpack and a Yankees baseball cap with the brim turned backwards. This was our drug pony. He stopped close enough to the tuc tuc to shake hands, which was what he proceeded to do, but his outstretched palm contained our delivery. It disappeared into Cody's hip pocket.

"Have you seen this one before?" I whispered.

"No." Cody got out. I quickly followed without knowing any more detail of his business plan. Was he improvising now? He kept one hand on the delivery kid's arm, and bent over into the tuc tuc with a fifty Q note in the other.

"Go now," he said to the driver, "we are finished, so thank you." He slid the note into the kid's shirt pocket. With a look of nervous enlightenment, he sped away. Cody and I now stood with one hand on each of the drug pony's wrists. Beads of sweat were breaking out in streams that collected in rivulets over his eyes.

"I never carry any money, and what you paid inside will go to my *jefe*," he said, "my boss, by its own way. I do not touch it. You have to realize that. It's only common sense." He was nodding vigorously as if to convince himself.

"Sure," Cody said, without releasing his wrist. "But now I have something more to say for your *jefe*. I have a business deal for him. Of course, he is a man meriting great respect here, and we wish to acknowledge that first. But where I come from there is suddenly a business opening for a person of his stature. That is why I have come here, because we wish to be connected to the source of our product." Cody watched as the delivery kid's eyes widened. "I will say the name for you, but you can not say it again to anyone else except the *jefe* himself when you arrive to give him this message in confidence." The kid was both nodding and breathing hard as Cody said the awesome word.

"*Chicago*. It makes this place look like Podunk Corners, Iowa. I need someone big, do you understand, someone with experience to help me there. And I need a source for some important supply. Not just trinkets like what you brought me."

The drug pony nodded vigorously as if he knew exactly what that meant. His eyes shifted around the street to see who might be witnessing this. So did mine. It struck me that the few people in view were elaborately paying no attention to this encounter. Without exception they were all moving away from us.

"Take that message to your boss," Cody said. "We'll be at the Dugu Bar this afternoon for what? Maybe two hours. If I don't hear from him, I will know who else to take this offer to, OK? I have heard there is someone over the border in Belize who is very important in this business. And he is not so far away. A person who knows the good seed."

We watched the kid spin off down the street on his superannuated Raleigh, headed north toward the densely overgrown hills. The purple backpack danced on his shoulders.

"Belize?" I said. "What do we know about Belize?"

"Nothing, but it has to be, so I was only guessing."

"Working the probabilities," I said. "Who are you expecting to show up next?"

"Not the chief himself, of course."

"It'll be some death squad crew leader looking for another couple of notches in his belt," I said, wishing again that I had a gun too.

"That's why we're not going to be at the Dugu Bar this afternoon, or ever. We just want to watch them line up their troops and see what we're coming up against."

We hiked back toward the hotel at a pace that fit the temperature. In six or seven minutes we reached La Casa del Pan, which offered cakes and sandwiches and pizzas from a blue frame building with a red tile roof over the porch. We climbed the two steps from the street and sat down at a small round table screened partly from the street by a trio of desperate palms.

The menu didn't offer any beer, but for the price of two lemonades we got to study the front of the Dugu Bar to see what might develop. Like most restaurants in Latin America, the Casa del Pan wouldn't bring your bill until you asked for it.

It took no more than forty-five minutes before a black Hummer pulled up, turned around in the street, and stopped in front of the Dugu Bar. Even the tires were knobby and aggressive. The bar was at a slight angle to us and through the open door I glimpsed a startled flicker of movement inside. Then, from behind the building, a figure running like he'd been shot from a cannon passed through an open space and disappeared behind the next shop. I recognized him as the waiter, or possibly the owner, who had served us earlier.

"Bingo," Cody said softly. We both arranged our chairs to be more fully screened by the dusty foliage.

The passenger door opened and a young buck walked around the front of the car to open the driver's door. He was wearing an olive drab sleeveless tee shirt and khaki pants above tall polished boots. The holster on his hip was too big to ignore.

The man who emerged from the driver's seat was tall and slender with long graying hair. It formed graceful waves over his ears. Looking close to fifty, he was wearing a pale blue shirt under a white linen vest, very lightweight. Most people don't wear white linen before Memorial Day, and it was still a few days off. I know that's an old rule. Who knows what people do now, especially in Guatemala for an occasion like this?

"Looks like a cool hand," Cody whispered. "See the bulge on his belt?"

The kid locked the car and they went onto the Dugu Bar porch. Three minutes later he came back and set down two beers and two glasses on a tray with napkins. There was no sign of the owner; he was probably already in Belize by then, still shaking. Along the street for two blocks not a soul was in sight. *High Noon*, I thought. I felt like I could hear my watch ticking.

They did not speak as they sat there staring at the street. The kid had his arms crossed but the older man sat in a perfectly relaxed Zen-like position, his hands flat on the table. I was waiting for them to spot us at the Casa del Pan, but it seemed like they were expecting a street approach. And they were ready.

"The pony boy would've described us when he got there," I said.

"He was extremely upset, and not a good witness. But that's why we're across the street now, undercover."

"What do we do?"

"The rule book is unclear for situations like this. The answers mostly involve calling in backup, whatever is close."

"Great. That would be a long distance call at best, or does that mean Maya unarmed in a short skirt?"

"Probably not this time," he said. "Although it has worked for us before. But even flirting has its limits."

"She would never admit that."

Cody and I sat there and finished our lemonades. Because most of the players weren't onstage yet, we were in no hurry. Neither were the friends of Lionel Merchant across the street. I couldn't help but notice that they weren't speaking to each other. Had they already said everything they had to say? Or were they working through an established procedure? Better yet, had they already said goodbye to each other? It didn't seem like it.

"It might be time to shake them up a little," Cody said, since nothing else had. "We don't want them getting too complacent."

"Sure. But how?"

"What if they need some help?"

"Why would they?"

"What if they suddenly felt vulnerable?"

"As if. I feel vulnerable unarmed just watching with only two of them."

He stood up. "Wait here and don't move. I'm going to shoot out one of their tires. Then they'll need some help."

"Won't that tell them where we are?" But Cody was already gone, slipping off the porch into the interior, through the kitchen, and gone. I tried to recall how many bullets he'd been able to buy. Was it only twenty-one? And now we were going to double or triple the forces lined up against us, and on their own turf. I had never had any cop training, mine was only common sense. I was glad Maya had gone back to the hotel for this. Sometimes her instincts were nearly perfect. She would most certainly live longer than I did and inherit a ton of unsold paintings.

By my watch two minutes and four seconds had passed before I heard the shot. I was looking at the Hummer, and the front tire on the driver's side sagged and settled with no other audible effect. But at the gunshot sound, our pals across the street were both on their feet.

"Years of required annual target practice," Cody said a minute later as he settled back into his seat. "It pays off in times like this." Across the street the two Merchant soldiers were keenly watching the thoroughfare in both directions. Nothing moved.

"But what did that get us?" I said, not liking the tone of my own voice.

"Now they're immobile."

"Great, but only their car is. They can still run as fast as we can. If that's immobility, then why did we start this?"

"OK, it's because we want to see what we're up against. I thought I said that."

"What if they're much bigger than we are?"

"Don't we already know that? Think about how big they really are."

I nodded. "And for the first time, we will see what they really have, against what we think they have."

"Right, and then we'll have a plan, rather than winging it nonstop."

I nodded slowly. "Like we are fucking now only winging it."

"But what happens when those heavily muscular guys call for help? Do they get the next lower rank sent in? Never. They get the next echelon upward. I'm hoping we'll see the *jefe* now very soon."

"So you've done this before. Great." Sometimes enthusiasm can be infectious, but not always.

Twenty-two minutes after the sudden tire failure on the Hummer, another black Hummer pulled up, swung around to face north just as the first one had, and stopped behind it. It was different in only one detail; on the driver's door was a gold logo about a foot in diameter. A heavily embellished M exactly like the one Maya had taken back to the hotel with her from the bank in Guatemala City. Two men jumped out gripping the same kind of machine pistols we'd seen all over the country. Their bulletproof vests were black. I've heard that Kevlar can be oppressive on a warm day, which this one was increasingly becoming by measurable degrees.

No one else emerged from behind the darkened glass, but the motor was still running, and so was the air conditioning.

"And here, I believe, is el *jefe*," Cody said. "I assume the windows are also bulletproofed."

"Are you getting ahead of yourself?"

"As always, but ready is better than dead."

"Just what are we expecting to get from this?"

He gave me a frank look. "This will yield an

undefended castle with the drawbridge in the lowered position."

"And the troops?"

He gave me a cynical grin. "Why, I believe the troops are all deployed by now around their fearless leader. The one who has not yet chosen to show his face in the coming fracas."

CHAPTER TWENTY

After we paid our tiny bill it wasn't hard to slip out the back of the bread cafe. While there wasn't an alley behind that row, it was still possible to go from shop to shop, often by way of small back yards where they kept their garbage cans. We raised a few eyebrows but no one challenged us. Not long afterward we emerged into a side street out of view of the Dugu Bar. We were standing in front of another restaurant, the Bahia Azul, a place with blue cloth awnings and a lot of detail. Half a block down a tuc tuc was approaching us. It appeared to be empty. Cody put his arm up and the headlight flickered in response.

"How much money have you got?" he said.

I scanned my wallet. "About twelve hundred quetzales."

"And I've got nine hundred, so together that's what...about two hundred eighty-five dollars or so? That should be enough."

When we settled in the back the driver turned.

He had an interesting scar that went from his right ear down his neck for about three inches. Two crude stiches had held it together while it healed in a graphic undisciplined ridge, and the earlobe was missing with a ragged edge along the bottom. It looked more like teeth marks than a cut line from a knife or razor. Cody gave him a steady gaze.

"You look like you're not afraid to take a chance."

He didn't smile. "Been there before a coupla times. What do you got?"

"Just a ride, same as you do all day."

"But you goin' someplace hot, I think."

"Right."

"Only one place here like that."

"The man called the Merchant."

"Sure. He the man, all right. You won't get into the house, but there's a guest cottage at the edge of the property. I can get you that far, if you're serious. I can see you got a gun. One might not be enough, though."

"How much?" I said, knowing that these bills are never paid in Oreos or Doritos. It would be coin of the realm.

The driver pursed his lips. Through the mirror, his eyes tried to read us, each in turn. I like to think neither of us is that easy to peg, but you never know. This guy had obviously been around.

"Two thousand Q."

A shrewd guess. That would leave us with a hundred left over for the return trip, but we probably weren't coming back anyway, at least in a tuc tuc, even if we could get one out there again to pick us up.

"You're on," Cody said.

I leaned back in the seat and texted Maya about the new plan. It wasn't going to be her idea of a fun time anyway. As we rounded the corner onto the main street going north I turned and looked through the tiny oval back window to see the two Hummers still positioned in front of the Dugu Bar, just waiting for us to make another move on them.

Six blocks further we left the ragged edges of Livingston. The road soon narrowed to a single lane and the foliage thickened into jungle. Every hundred meters or so was a place to pull off if you ran into someone coming the other way. It probably wasn't likely.

"How far is it?" Cody said, leaning forward.

"Twelve kilometers."

"You've taken people out here before?"

"Sure, but usually Mr. Merchant knows about it ahead of time. Then it costs much less."

He asked no more questions, which was just as well. At this point in other cases Cody would've been checking and possibly oiling his gun, but that would've alarmed the driver. We would've been going over what we expected, but that would also have alarmed the driver and us as well. I didn't think we spoke any languages that he didn't.

In fact, I had no idea what we might expect. The best prospect was that Darren Hall was there, that he was under diminished guard because we'd drawn the staff into town, and we'd be able to somehow spirit him away with the application of one old military side arm and twenty uncertain bullets. There was precious little reason to think this. We only rode on through the jungle at about twenty-five kilometers an hour as the sweat poured off our faces. We were climbing steadily, but not steeply.

The tuc tuc came out onto a ridge overlooking a shallow valley. Three neat but small garden patches were visible, interrupting the jungle. They would've had the benefit of whatever soil erosion had been deposited there from the slopes. The road we were on threaded past them and climbed slowly up the other side.

Two buildings were visible. The closest sat somewhat down from the summit on the other side. It was done in pink stucco with a long verandah facing the valley. Three graceful arches supported the tile roof.

The tuc tuc paused. "There on the lower part is the guest house. I can only go that far because they will fire on us if we come closer. Up to that place they can't see us as we come from the bottom of the valley."

"Good idea," Cody said. "We'll get off there. Maybe they'll offer us a Planter's Punch. Is it usually occupied?"

"We can't know this. In the past it is for people doing business with Mr. Merchant. Now, who knows? It could be a big surprise."

"I hope so," I said, wishing I at least had a knife, or even a sharp stick. Steel-toed shoes would've helped, too, but no, I'd worn my sandals because they offered a lot of ventilation.

Four minutes later we pulled into a gravel drive in the shadow of the guesthouse verandah. The driver, whose name we had never heard—surely that was no accident—accepted two thousand Q from us and disappeared with a satisfied smile. We'd arrived in the Merchant domain.

Five steps up from where we stood two sets of closed and covered French doors gave access to the terrace, even as an air conditioner hummed in the background. Someone was staying there.

"How do we do this?" I said. "I don't think our visit should start with the homicide squad cop knock."

Hands on his hips, he looked at me. "OK, you're thinking subtle and friendly. Like we're lost hikers from a Swiss elder hostel group."

"Why not? I've still got a little German left from college. We're wondering if they have a local terrain map and a couple glasses of cool water to send us on our healthy way. Meanwhile, your gun is slyly tucked into the back of your pants instead of on your hip like that."

"Tougher to reach there in a pinch, and there's always the risk of shooting your ass off if your grip isn't just right."

"But it's also about not starting a war if we can help it."

"You're saying we just want information."

"Then why don't y'all come inside and get some?" This came from the blond woman leaning over the rail behind us. Cody reached for his hip as we turned in an instant to confront Barbara Watt.

CHAPTER TWENTY-ONE

Even with our mixed history, I'm almost always glad to see Barbara, but this most unexpected encounter had its own special glow. When she opened the guesthouse door, Ixobel Bak was unmistakably standing behind her shoulder, six inches shorter. The two thousand quetzales cab fare suddenly seemed well spent. What was less encouraging was that both women had the index finger of their right hand vertically crossing their lips. Barbara waved to us to come through the house to a small garden pavilion ten meters away before she spoke.

"Do you know where you are? I can't imagine that you could get here by accident. How did you find me?"

"We didn't mean to find you, we wanted to find Lionel Merchant," Cody said. "The question is why it was also you."

Without responding, Barbara introduced us to Ixobel Bak in a whisper. She didn't mention Ixobel's connection to Darren Hall as we followed them outside to the more distant shaded terrace. "I'm not so trusting of the interior of that lovely guesthouse, since Lionel offers it to a number people he supplies on a wholesale basis. I think he likes to listen in on their conversations. Let's just talk out here in a lower tone of voice." There we would be somewhat screened by the chatter of birds and the flutter of insects.

"Of course," said Cody, giving a warm look to Ixobel, which she deserved, even though I thought her hair was pulled back so tight it elongated the shape of her eyes. That was just her style, and our impression from the Bernard Emerson photo was affirmed. She appeared to be intense and intelligent.

"We are both here because my *novio* (fiancé), Darren, was kidnapped by Lionel Merchant."

"Did he have a better choice for you?" Cody said.

I thought this was a bit improvisational, but we had come a long way at great expense, and finding them was the last thing either of us had expected.

"No. But Darren has always been rather a wild child."

"Ah," I said. This was no surprise, but it left me wanting more detail. "And that is what you like about him?" A shot in the dark, but sometimes they'll hit something you didn't see.

She blushed. "Well, yes, most of the time. You

must understand that I come from a very conservative background. My father is a priest in Antigua. Not in the cathedral, of course, but a big church nonetheless. As children he kept a close rein on all of us in order to give no scandal." This was entirely in Spanish.

"Well, I can see how that works." What! No wonder the maid in Antigua had been cagey about Ixobel's presence.

Barbara seized my hand. "I can understand how this is making you nervous. Can I get you two a drink?"

I didn't have to look at my watch again. "Of course." She didn't move. "You didn't bring Maya?"

"She wanted to catch up on some bookkeeping," Cody said. "Are you saying Darren is here?"

Ixobel nodded. "Lionel has him locked in a room in the big house while we negotiate this problem. As you can observe, this is extremely sad for us. Lionel is very busy, so we do not always have a discussion when we wish to. Besides, he is not well, so that is also part of the problem."

"What's wrong with him?" I said.

"No one knows for certain, but he is sometimes in a chair with wheels, and he bends over like he cannot breathe."

Barbara snorted here, and not in sympathy. "What I have heard from several sources is that the man has put the sale price of an entire house in town up his nose."

Of course, real estate had been part of some of our earlier cases, if not exactly in this manner. "Have you called the police?"

"Lionel owns the police. This is a poor town, Se-ñor Zacher, so he pays their salaries and their pensions. Everyone is grateful, since it is now an orderly place to live. Not all of the Caribbean is."

"So I shouldn't try to steal a pig here," Cody said.

"Better not."

This made sense. How else could Merchant's people still be parked in front of the Dugu Bar lofting machine pistols in their hands? At least, I hoped they were still there doing that. Part of being a successful crook was looking like a benefactor. Think of Al Capone paying for the baptism of infants in his neighborhood. I glanced at my watch.

"What's at issue here?" I said. "Tell us the bottom line. I don't think we have much time."

Barbara gave us a frank look. "It's a hundred thousand dollars in ransom." She certainly had that available as small change. The issue had to be whether she saw any reason to spend it in this way.

"But I thought Lionel's business was more about drugs," I said, "and Darren is a scholar."

"In its effects, kidnapping is a highly visible event," said Cody, a little more sternly. "And unlike with drug use, there is usually an outraged victim with his family behind him." He was clearly thinking of our avuncular employer. "I'm not sure I can see why Merchant would get involved with a crime that has such a high profile. One that was likely to pull in embassies and even Interpol."

"But this really starts from a business deal that went sour," said Ixobel. "You probably don't know that Darren sometimes deals in antiquities. This country is full of them, and there are thousands more to be discovered. By training he was an anthropologist in his early career."

"I may have heard a rumor to that effect," I said, glancing at Barbara. "What is he doing now?"

"So I can tell you that Darren had recently come across a wonderful Mayan death mask in jade," said Ixobel, "from the seventh or eighth century, I do not know exactly. They are very rare, and few appear in private collections. He never told me how he got it, but it was connected with something he found out at Tikal. He had been there three times before like a tourist, because that is a place you would visit first and perhaps again in his field, but that last time he was there in the evening, with a small unusual group at twilight as he told me, and then he made a wonderful discovery that is still a secret. But it changed his life. I know this for certain."

"Then he offered no more detail?" I said.

"Only that a secret chamber was opened that evening. Maybe you can ask him when he is freed."

"But how did he get possession of the mask itself?" Cody said. "I assume he didn't get it that evening in the ancient city."

"No. And he did not tell me that. He believes that women should not know everything about business."

Now I wished that Maya, as our CEO, had come along. She would've had a much better response than I did to a woman. Had a man said this, I would've known better what to say, but I couldn't read Ixobel's response to it. I wonder if she minded being out of the loop on Darren's activities.

"Now wait a minute before this goes on any farther," said Barbara. "We have the mask here now, so that's not the problem. It's in the drawer of the hallway table you passed as you came through our little guesthouse. Darren had a nice wooden case made for it."

A look of alarm crossed Cody's face. "And that's a good place for it because no one would ever think to look there?"

"No! It's a good place because it's a skillful reproduction that's only worth about nine hundred dollars, which is why we are now here and so are you. Ixobel does not believe the mask is an expert copy. Having handled more Mayan jade artifacts new and old than anyone I know, I saw right away when I handled it what it was.

While it's a sophisticated piece of design, and it doesn't duplicate any known death mask, I'm absolutely sure it's no more than two or three years old, and probably more like two or three months."

I was starting to come onto the truth of this now. "So Lionel Merchant spotted it too? Is that the problem?"

"Yes." Barbara was not looking at Ixobel, who had folded her arms and was pacing off the back wall of the garden pavilion in a grimly measured step in a pattern as tight as her hairline. These were things she probably didn't care to hear.

"OK," said Cody. "Did it go something like this? Darren gets an idea that there is a missing mask from the cluster of burials at Tikal. He hires an expert jade artisan to make a speculative copy. Then he has a falling out about price with that same maker in Antigua, for whom it took more time than he thought it would, which led to an ugly scene."

I watched Ixobel's reaction as he said this, expecting an eruption, but she only stopped and turned away. This of course had been Darren's rough night in Antigua that Bernard had told us about. It had happened at The Blue Gazelle. I suddenly wished the old man were here to see this meeting. He would soon realize how well the Zacher Agency earned its keep.

"Which led Darren to demand more money

from Lionel Merchant," said Barbara, "who had already agreed to a price of $100,000. When Darren showed up here with the mask, saying that its quality and condition justified a higher price, Lionel saw it first as a shakedown, and then on a closer examination, as a speculive reproduction, a rip off. That was much worse."

The further we got into this the more it looked to me like a negotiation more than a confrontation. So what if our victim had been more than a little shady? Can't we all reform? Bernard was certainly a distinguished gentleman whose main consideration was making sense of his declining years and protecting his family. Isn't there a way to come out at least even for honest people on both sides? It made me yearn for the old West of the movies, where people wore black hats or white, and they acted accordingly.

"So Lionel locked him up," Cody said.

"Yes, and gave us the mask when we got here, saying that he would release Darren for the same price he wanted for the jade. He had allowed Darren to contact us. We've only been able to meet with Lionel twice, and there's been no movement."

"What kind of leverage do you have?" I said.

"Listen," Cody said. "This is all theory and speculation. I don't care who wants what. If you're not going to fork over the money, or at least not that much, we'd better get Darren sprung and on the road before they come back. What is the entrance of the house like?"

"It's a conventional Latin American four square two story colonial style house. It has a big interior courtyard, rather dense and overgrown." Barbara's hands described it.

"How about the entrance? I assume you've been there to negotiate?"

"Yes, Lionel doesn't get around that easily and there isn't a road directly between this house and his. It's only a jungle path so in a car you have to loop around a bit. The entrance is a thick plank door with a rectangular slot in it. You hand your cash in and the gatekeeper hands out the package of weed, or whatever it is."

"So the gatekeeper looks out at the customer through that slot?" I said.

"Yes. It's the only opening."

I looked at Cody. "Then we just shoot him in the face when he looks at us."

"You'd have to be awfully quick. I'm not sure I'm that fast anymore, and if it doesn't come off that way the first time, then he just covers the slot and walks away. We need a way of holding him down while I pick the lock." He looked at Barbara and Ixobel, who had just now rejoined us. "Do you have any meds? Anything at all? Something in a box or a pharmacy bag?"

"I have some Motrin in a box," Barbara said.

"Terrific! Pack it up, we're going up the hill."

CHAPTER TWENTY-TWO

It might have been a hundred meters up a twisting path to a small courtyard in front of the white colonial headquarters of Lionel Merchant. To the left was a triple garage complex that was served by a road that went up to the crest of the hill. We couldn't see any more as we approached. In a way I wanted to meet him in the flesh, to humiliate him, but his position as a semi-invalid murderous drug lord left me equivocal as to what I would do to him if we survived to get that close to him.

More important was getting away with our Agency objective met: the release of Darren Hall. In the detective business we had always stayed away from the drug cartels in México. Those were business crimes, and as such, were a better issue for the police.

The path was not difficult if you enjoyed the temperature and humidity both approaching triple digits. I could imagine Cody's .45 automatic rusting into a solid block of unresponsive steel on his hip.

We stopped just inside the thick edge of the

foliage with the sweat streaming off our faces. The entry was directly ahead of us, but we stayed in the shadows and circled around to approach the entrance from the far left. Barbara had been exact in her description. At a height of about a meter and a half, or a little less, was a rectangular slot about six inches high by twelve wide. The door was otherwise blank but for a handle and deadbolt lock. A person inside could bend slightly to look through it, or reach his hand out at shoulder height to collect money or deliver a package of drugs. Thanks to Barbara, we had brought our own.

"Do we knock?" I said quietly.

"No," she said. "I have the cell number to call, but what do I say?"

"It's a drug deal," Cody said. "But this time it's a delivery for them because we're the suppliers. Dial the number and say you have meds for Darren, and he has to have them for his blood pressure. When Merchant locked him up he had only a few days supply in his pocket. He didn't expect to be gone so long. Now it's an emergency. He's worth nothing to them dead."

I want to believe we reached the entrance unobserved. The little slot did not open to view us and no one called out, although we could be easily observed from the upper floor. But after the military assembly outside of the Dugu Bar, how many troops could still be left inside the mansion? The main force would've been drawn off to face the false threat in Livingston, and what remained was only routine guard duty at home. I was hoping it was reduced to only one soldier.

While the rest of us stood with our backs flattened against the walls, Barbara faced the door and dialed the number. She spoke in rapid Spanish to someone who answered almost immediately. While I counted the seconds I thought it was interesting that Cody did not yet have his hand on his gun.

Ixobel had lost her skeptical look and was now hunched petrified further down the wall, her hands gripping each other behind her back. While I had no idea what was coming, it still did not look like a shootout.

With a determined look, Barbara shut off her phone and shoved it in the back pocket of her jeans. "We're all set."

"Get out the meds and have them ready, but make him reach out for them the length of his hand," Cody whispered to her.

She pulled a small Farmacia Guadalajara bag from her front pocket, but didn't open it. The white plastic outlined the box inside without revealing specifically what it was.

On the other side of the thick plank door, the cover opened, and a hand shot out ten inches to receive the bag of meds.

I have mentioned before how big Cody is. He's

not as young and fast as he once was, but you still don't want to get too close to him in a confrontation. I only had an instant to notice a tattooed letter on each knuckle before he seized the offered hand and yanked it forward to slam the body on the other side full force into the thick plank door.

What stays with me most now, as I make these notes almost two months later, is the bone-snapping impact of that gatekeeper's head on the other side of the door, almost like a melon hitting concrete. Cody of course handed that dangling arm to me, saying, "Don't let this drop back through the slot. Keep it all the way down on the door to hold him up on the other side by his armpit while I pick this lock."

We paused for a moment, listening for the sound of running feet, but there was no one else coming. In an instant Cody had pulled the picks out and was hard at work. Probably the loudest sound as I stood there leaning against that limp arm on the door was from the drops of sweat rolling down my face. As I pulled down on it, the arm offered no movement. The body on the other side must've been just as limp.

"Good lock," Cody muttered quietly. Barbara and Ixobel remained plastered against the wall a few feet further down. I was also listening for the sound of tires on gravel.

With a subtle click the lock yielded and Cody

pushed the door open inch by inch, moving the unconscious body with it. I released the arm and it was immediately pulled back through. He turned to Barbara. "Why not wait out of sight just inside the trees and call me if a car turns up? I wouldn't mind having a little warning."

She and Ixobel moved off with an eager nod.

Inside I was expecting to find a young recruit lying on the floor of the entry but it was an older man of about sixty. Cody located a stable pulse on his neck, but the irregular bruise on one side of his face looked dangerous. I suppose every job has its risks, and his may have paid better than most here. The man had a .38 revolver in a belt holster and I seized it. The cylinder was full. Life was good, even if slightly too risky. In his left pants pocket I also found a set of car keys, so I took them too. We had as yet no plan for getting back to Livingston, and if there was still a vehicle on the property, that would be our ticket out. Cody clipped the unconscious man's hands together behind him with a set of disposable restraints and we moved further inside.

As Barbara had described, the interior was the standard colonial floor plan; four two-story galleries facing a large courtyard full of trees and vines with an antique stone fountain in the center. It was flanked by two macaws that made no comment on our presence. Between the arch supports the ornate iron railings were exquisite in their detail. The floors were made from squares of porous black volcanic stone, not tile. No one else was in view. We began to walk down the first loggia on the right, pounding on each locked door, yelling the name, "Darren Hall!" Most were unlocked. I was pleased to have my own gun as I watched Cody's back.

A full circuit of the main floor brought us no response so we climbed the steps to the next level. Then, on the back wall, Cody's cop knock brought a similar pounding from the other side of the door. "Darren?" He yelled again. A muted voice said, "Yes! Yes! I'm in here!" Cody pulled the lock picks out again.

When the door flew open it did not surprise me that the man rushing out was a mess. His white shirt was filthy and he was barefoot, a condition most people did not prefer in the presence of scorpions, and he smelled as if he hadn't bathed in days. Reaching out toward us, he began to cry with relief.

"Quick," I said, seizing his hand to keep him from running off, "we have Ixobel outside and we need to move before Merchant comes back. Do you have anything to bring along?"

He only shook his head. "Oh my God, oh my God," he kept saying. His kinky red hair was now ballooned untethered around his head. "Who sent you to do this? How did you even know? Oh my God!"

"We can talk about that later," said Cody roughly. "Now let's get the hell out of here." When we ran back toward the door Darren was limping. We could get into why after we left the estate.

When we emerged into the blazing sun of the courtyard outside, Barbara and Ixobel were waiting at the third garage stall. The doors were open to reveal a well-used Ford pickup, red in color, and none too clean. With a wrinkle to her nose Ixobel ran up and embraced Darren. He was still mumbling.

I drew the car keys from the door guard out of my pocket and climbed inside the pickup. The engine came to life and I pulled out of the garage. It was a crew cab, seating five or six, so everyone found a space inside. Cody pulled the door shut behind us and got into the back seat. He must've been thinking that if Merchant didn't immediately realize the pickup was gone that might buy us a little time.

We flew off on the ridge road. Barbara was next to me in front and Ixobel was connecting with Darren. I found the unpaved loop that went down to the guest-house and pulled up in its shadow two minutes later.

"Quick, get everything as fast as you can!" Cody said in a coarse whisper. Leaving the truck doors open, we all ran inside.

CHAPTER TWENTY-THREE

What we did not expect to see in the guest-house was an extremely short Guatemalan man standing just inside the hallway. In his arms, clutched to his chest, was the mahogany box that must have contained the jade funeral mask. His face was blank and his eyes wide open, as if he were just as surprised as we were. He was not armed.

"Give me that box!" Darren leaped forward toward the man, who turned away but did not retreat. From behind us came a muffled, almost strangled sound. I swung around to see Bernard Emerson, one arm around Ixobel's neck and the other holding a gun to her temple. We all froze in place.

"Take it easy now, Bernard," Cody said, his hands raised to shoulder level. "Just take it easy. This is all under control. No one needs to get hurt."

"Of course it is. We will start, if you don't mind, by having Ivan collect your gun or guns from you. Any other movement will result in me putting a bullet through this young woman's head. You cannot possibly move fast enough to change that outcome." He smiled at us, Cody and me in particular. "You of the Paul Zacher Agency have done your jobs well. While I think that at 10,000 U. S. dollars I have paid you enough, rest assured that I shall give you the highest recommendations to anyone who asks, with the single reservation that you have a tendency to think your job is over slightly before it really is. Put that wonderful mask and the guns in the SUV, Ivan."

"This was your dream," said Cody in a low tone of voice as Ivan edged past us and went out the door.

"Always. I had discovered from my research that there had to be a missing death mask from Tikal and when I heard Darren was going after it, I knew I had to be part of the program, no matter what it cost. As you can imagine, I have followed his career, and this piece will be the crown of my collection."

I heard a vehicle pull up on the gravel outside. "Ready boss," Ivan said a moment later. He appeared behind Emerson's shoulder, another gun trained on us.

"You will excuse me, then," said our client. "I do not wish you to die at the hands of Lionel Merchant, but all the same, wait a bit before you leave here."

He turned and left. I took a couple of steps forward as I heard his car doors close. He and Ivan were leaving in the white Toyota SUV that we had seen several times on the road. I turned to look at Darren.

Ixobel had her arms tightly around him. I couldn't help but be moved.

"I'm very sorry, Darren. It must be terribly humiliating to be betrayed by your uncle like that, your only remaining family." I said this with heart-felt sympathy, and I know that was clear in my voice. I would've also hugged him but he smelled too bad.

Darren Hall looked at me in utter surprise. "What do you mean? I never saw that man before in my entire life. Who is he?"

JOHN SCHERBER

TWILIGHT AT TIKAL